彩色版

金字塔學習法
The Pyramid Method
自然易學美語發音法

Phonics Book

循序漸進建立
發音基礎概念

Step by Step

Building Phonics

The Natural and Easy Way
for Learning English Phonics

Geoffrey S. Ricciardi
Jih-Xian Lin

2

AQUARIUS PUBLISHING

The Natural and Easy Way for Learning
English Phonics-The Pyramid Method. First Edition 1996
Second Edition 2010, Revised (Color Version)

Illustrator: Chio - Der Liu; Wei-Wen Lin; Deo
Cover design: Aiko; Robert G. Gavin Jr.; Deo
Editor: John Grimes

Special thanks to: Pai-Chun Lin; Chia-Chen Chang

國家圖書館　出版品預行編目資料

自然易學美語發音法：金字塔學習法
The Natural and Easy Way for Learning English Phonics:
The Pyramid Method /雷家輔(Geoffrey S. Ricciardi)，林季嫻　編著
－彩色第一版－花蓮市：2010〔民99〕
冊：　　　　公分
ISBN 957-98913-1-1 (第1冊：平裝)
ISBN 957-98913-3-8 (第2冊：平裝)
1.英國語語－語音
805.14　　　　　　　　　　　　　87017012

自然易學美語發音法—金字塔學習法2

編著者：Geoffrey S. Ricciardi (雷家輔)・林季嫻
校閱：J.Grimes
美術編輯：林薇文・林郁潔 ・羅凱文・劉秋德・雷家輔
製版印刷：設計一百工作室
發行人：林季嫻
發行所：宏泉文教出版社
登記證：局版台業字第0360號
地址：花蓮市970國興二街97號
電話：(03)836-0039
傳真：(03)836-0127
彩色版一刷：2010 年1月
劃撥帳號：06666567
戶名：宏泉文教出版社
E-mail：phoncards@hotmail.com(中文)
　　　　aquapub@ms31.hinet.net(English)
ISBN 957-98913-3-8(平裝)

ABCDEFGHIJKLMNOPQRSTUVWXYZ

Table of Contents

"Building Phonics Step by Step"

abcdefghijklmnopqrstuvwxyz

目錄

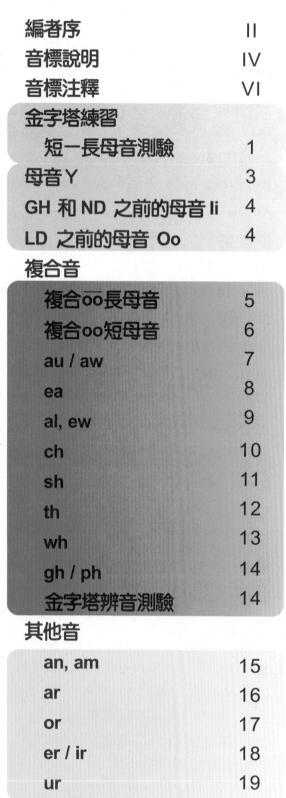

『循序漸進　建立發音基礎概念』

Preface

These books have been carefully designed after many years of teaching English to non-native speakers. They are intended to make English phonics easy to understand and pronounce. The advantage of phonics is that it uses no symbols outside the alphabet itself and may be used as an alternative to "IPA"-based phonetic systems such as "K.K.", "Jones", etc.

In these books, the main focus is on the rules that are used for learning English pronunciation, similar to the way native speakers learn in the United States. However, these books have been adapted for non-native speakers, and if followed correctly will make learning English phonics easy and fun. They can be used in conjunction with other books such as readers or series grammar books.

The idea of using a pyramid comes from the concept of a good foundation. A good foundation is needed to build a solid pyramid. The same idea applies to learning English. If a solid "phonetic" foundation is established early, then you can continue to build on that foundation and your English skills will improve. These books are especially designed to give you that solid foundation so you will want to continue practicing English throughout your life.

"Building Phonics Step by Step"

編者序

本書是作者集多年在非英語系國家之教學經驗精心編寫而成的。本書的主旨在使英語發音簡單易懂且易學。使用自然發音法的長處在於：它以英文字母為發音符號，而不須使用特殊符號。因此它可以是目前通用的發音法中，諸如**K.K.**音標及**Jones**音標之外的另一項選擇。

本書強調英語發音的規則，美國的小學生也以同樣的方法學習發音。因此作者在編寫本書時也特別考慮到；這本書是以非英語系的學習者為對象，所以只要您以本書為藍本循序漸進的練習，相信各位將輕鬆快樂地學會英語發音。本書也可以配合其他教材一起使用，例如：英語讀本或文法教材。

使用金字塔的用意在說明穩固的基礎對於精通英語的重要性。就如同建造一座堅固的金字塔必自底層著手，因此讀者在學習英語之初就應具備基礎英語發音概念。本書著眼於幫助讀者建立發音基礎，對讀者日後學習英語將有莫大的益處。

『循序漸進　建立發音基礎概念』

Pronunciation Guide

(PM) [KK]

Note: The symbols used for English pronunciation vary from one to another.

The Pyramid Method (PM) follows the standard format used by most American dictionaries and schools. The chart below compares

The Pyramid Method with K.K. to show how much easier

The Pyramid Method is to use and understand.   A= alternative

Example Spellings 例字		PM	A	K.K.	Example Spellings 例字		PM	A	K.K.
hat	(hat)	a	ă	æ	hat	(hat)	h		h
hate	(hāt)	ā		e	whale	(hwāl)	hw		hw
wash	(wäsh) *1	ä	o	ɑ	kit	(kit)	i	ĭ	ɪ
car	(kär) *2	är		ɑr	kite	(kīt)	ī		aɪ
sauce draw	(sôs) (drô)	ô		ɔ	bird	(burd) *3	ʊr		ɝ
boy	(boi)	b		b	jeep	(jēp)	j		dʒ
cat face	(kat) (fās) see page 8	k s		k s	key	(kē)	k		k
church	(church)	ch		tʃ	leg	(leg)	l		l
dog	(däg) (dôg)	d		d	bell	(bel)	l		l
met	(met)	e	ĕ	ɛ	moon	(mōōn)	m		m
meet	(mēt)	ē		i	home	(hōm)	m		m
herd	(hurd) *3	ʊr		ɝ	nine	(nīn)	n		n
fish	(fish)	f		f	ten	(ten)	n		n
gate gym	(gāt) see page 12 (jim)	g j		g dʒ	sing	(siŋ)	ŋ	ng	ŋ

"Building Phonics Step by Step"

Building Phonics
The Pyramid Method
Step by Step

III

音標符號說明

(PM) [KK]

> **說明：**英語發音所使用的符號各系統之間略有差異。金字塔學習法（PM）使用最多美國字典與學校所採用的標準符號系統。下列比較金字塔學習法（PM）與 K.K.音標的圖表中顯示出；相對於 K.K.音標，金字塔學習法（PM）比較易於了解與使用，且符合使用字母本身為發音符號的原則。
>
> A＝替代符號

Example Spellings 例字		PM	A	K.K.	Example Spellings 例字		PM	A	K.K.
hot	(hät)	ä	ŏ	ɑ	thin bath	(thin)　*5 (bath)	th		θ
boat	(bōt)	ō		o	the father	(thə)　*5 (fä'thər)	th		ð
boy oil	(boi) (oil)	oi		ɔɪ	cut	(kut)	u	ŭ	ʌ
book	(book)	oo	ŏŏ	ʊ	cute	(kyōot)	yoo	ū	ju
zoo	(zōō)	ōō		u	nurse	(nʊrs)　*3	ʊr		ɝ
for all	(fôr)　*4 (ôl)	ôr ô		ɔɪ ɔ	van	(van)	v		v
out	(out)	ou		aʊ	web	(web)	w		w
pen	(pen)	p		p	box	(bäks)	ks		k s
quite	(kwīət)	kw		kw	yo-yo	(yō-yō)	y		j
road	(rōd)	r		r	zoo	(zōō)	z		z
chair	(cher)	r		r	pleasure	(plezh'ər)	zh		ʒ
sleep	(slēp)	s		s	ago item	(ə gō')　*6 (īt'əm)	ə		ə
ship fish	(ship) (fish)	sh		ʃ	quality	(kwäl'ə tē)	ə		ə
ten	(ten)	t		t	handsome focus	(han'səm) (fō'kəs)	ə		ə

『循序漸進　建立發音基礎概念』

Pronunciation Notes

*1. **ä** This symbol represents the "a"sound in the word **w<u>a</u>sh**.
It is sometimes referred to as the short **"o"** sound.

*2. **är** This symbol represents the "a" sound which is followed by **r** as in **c<u>ar</u>**.

*3. **ur** This symbol represents the sounds of **"er"**, **"ir"**, and **"ur"** when they are stressed as in **h<u>er</u>d**, **b<u>ir</u>d**, and **n<u>ur</u>se**.

ər This symbol represents the sounds of **"ar"**, **"er"**, and **"or"** when they are at the end of a word and not stressed, as in **doll<u>ar</u>**, **teach<u>er</u>**, and **doct<u>or</u>**.

*4. **ôr** This symbol represents the **"o"** sound which is followed by **r** as in **f<u>or</u>**.

ô This symbol also represents the sound of **"al"** as in **<u>al</u>l** and **t<u>al</u>k**.

*5. **th** This symbol represents the voiceless **"th"** sound as in **<u>th</u>in** and **ba<u>th</u>**.

_th_ This symbol represents the voiced **_"th"_** sound as in **<u>th</u>e** and **fa<u>th</u>er**.

*6. **ə** The symbol, called the schwa, represents the unstressed vowels in **<u>a</u>go**, it<u>e</u>m, qual<u>i</u>ty, hands<u>o</u>me, and foc<u>u</u>s.

★ Long Vowel Combination Chart ★

a	e	i	o	u
~a-e	~e-e	~i-e	~o-e	~u-e
~ai~	~ea~	~ie	~oa~	~ue
~ay	~ee~		~oe	
	~ey		~o	
	~e			

Building Phonics
The Pyramid Method
Step by Step

v

音標注釋

*1. **ä**   這個符號所代表的是 w<u>a</u>sh 中的母音 "a"，它在有些音標系統中被視為短母音 "o"。

*2. **är**   這個符號所代表的是：當 a 後面跟隨 r 時的發音，例如：c<u>ar</u>。

*3. **ʉr**   這個符號所代表的是 "er"、"ir" 和 "ur" 為重音節的母音時的發音，例如：h<u>er</u>d、b<u>ir</u>d 和 n<u>ur</u>se。

      ər   這個符號所代表的是：當 "ar"、"er" 和 "or" 在一個字或一個音節之尾，而且<u>不為重音之所在</u>時的發音，例如：doll<u>ar</u>、teach<u>er</u> 和 doct<u>or</u>。

*4. **ôr**   這個符號所代表的是：當 o 後面跟著 r 時的發音，例如：f<u>or</u>。

      ô   這個符號也代表了 "al" 的發音，例如：<u>all</u> 和 t<u>al</u>k。

*5. **th**   這個符號所代表的是無聲的 th 音，例如：<u>th</u>in 和 ba<u>th</u>。

      th   這個符號所代表的是有聲的 *th* 音，例如：<u>th</u>e 和 fa<u>th</u>er。

*6. **ə**   這個符號又叫做中性母音，其所代表的是：當 a、e、i、o 或 u 不為重音節母音時的發音，例如：<u>a</u>go、it<u>e</u>m、qual<u>i</u>ty、hands<u>o</u>me 和 foc<u>u</u>s。

★ 長母音組合表 ★

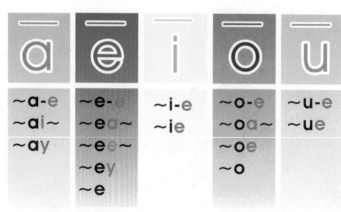

SHORT-LONG VOWEL TEST （短-長母音測驗）

Directions: Let's review the **short** and **long** vowel sounds. Listen for both sounds and put the words in the correct pyramid. After you finish, time yourself pronouncing the words by alternating the **short** and **long** sounds (examples: cap-cape, pip-pipe).

說明：注意聽並辨別長母音和短母音的不同。如果聽到含有短母音的字，就把這個字填入左邊的金字塔內。如果聽到含有長母音的字，就把它填入右邊的金字塔中。完成之後，將短母音的字和長母音的字交互著念，例如：**cap-cape** 或 **pip-pipe**。計算自己共花了多少時間唸完全部的字。

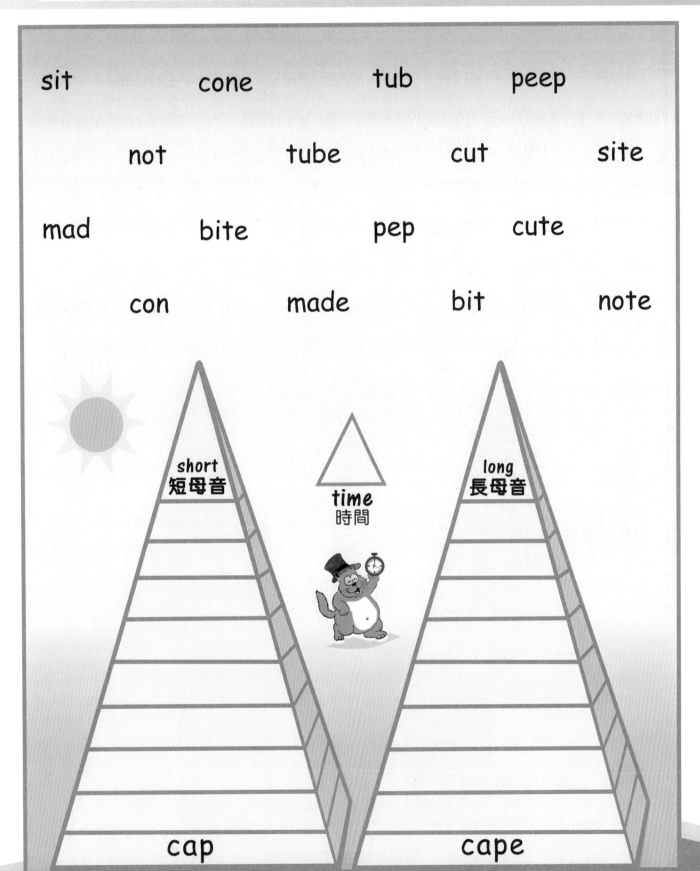

sit   cone   tub   peep

not   tube   cut   site

mad   bite   pep   cute

con   made   bit   note

short
短母音

time
時間

long
長母音

cap

cape

SHORT-LONG VOWEL TEST （短-長母音測驗）

Directions: Let's review the **short** and **long** vowel sounds. Listen for both sounds and put the words in the correct pyramid. After you finish, time yourself pronouncing the words by alternating the **short** and **long** sounds (examples: pip-pipe, cap-cape).

說明： 注意聽並辨別長母音和短母音的不同。如果聽到含有短母音的字，就把這個字填入左邊的金字塔內。如果聽到含有長母音的字，就把它填入右邊的金字塔中。完成之後，將短母音的字和長母音的字交互著念，例如：**pip-pipe** 或 **cap-cape**。計算自己共花了多少時間唸完全部的字。

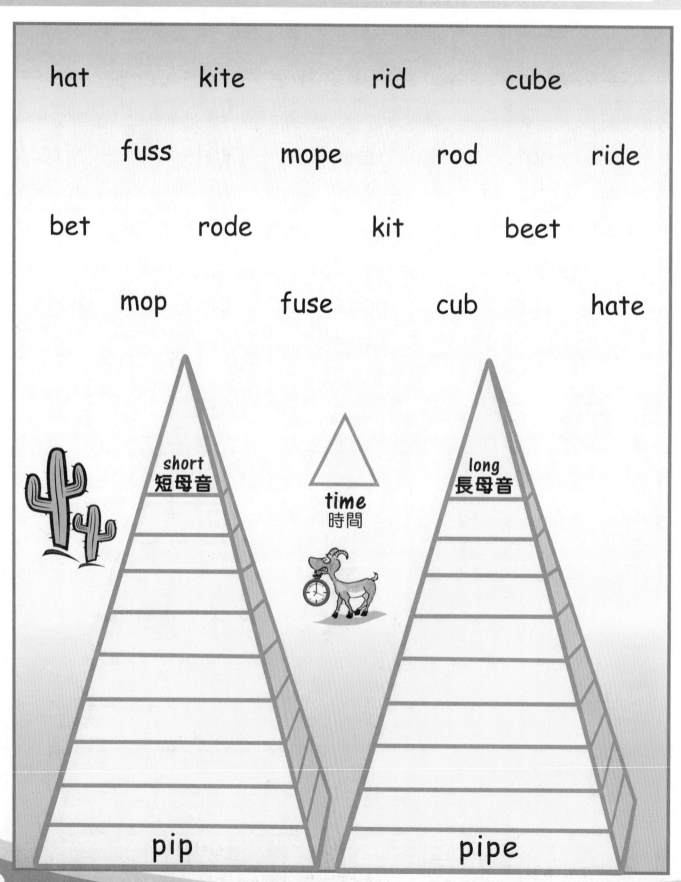

hat   kite   rid   cube

fuss   mope   rod   ride

bet   rode   kit   beet

mop   fuse   cub   hate

short 短母音

time 時間

long 長母音

pip

pipe

VOWEL Y (母音 Y)

★ **Rule 1:** When y is the only vowel at the <u>end</u> of a one-syllable word, y is <u>usually</u> pronounced as the **long " i " sound** (example: b<u>y</u>).

★ **規則 1：** 當 y 出現在單一音節字的結尾且 y 為唯一的母音，這時 y 通常發長母音 i 的發音。

★ **Rule 2:** When y is at the <u>end</u> of a word with more than one syllable, y is <u>usually</u> pronounced as the **long " e " sound** (example: baby).

★ **規則 2：** 當 y 出現在一個字的結尾且這個字有二個音節以上，這時 y 通常發長母音 e 的發音。

Directions: Listen and say the words and then write them in the correct pyramid.

說明： 注意聽並說出下列的字，將它們填入正確的金字塔中。左邊為 y 發長母音 i，右邊為 y 發長母音 e。

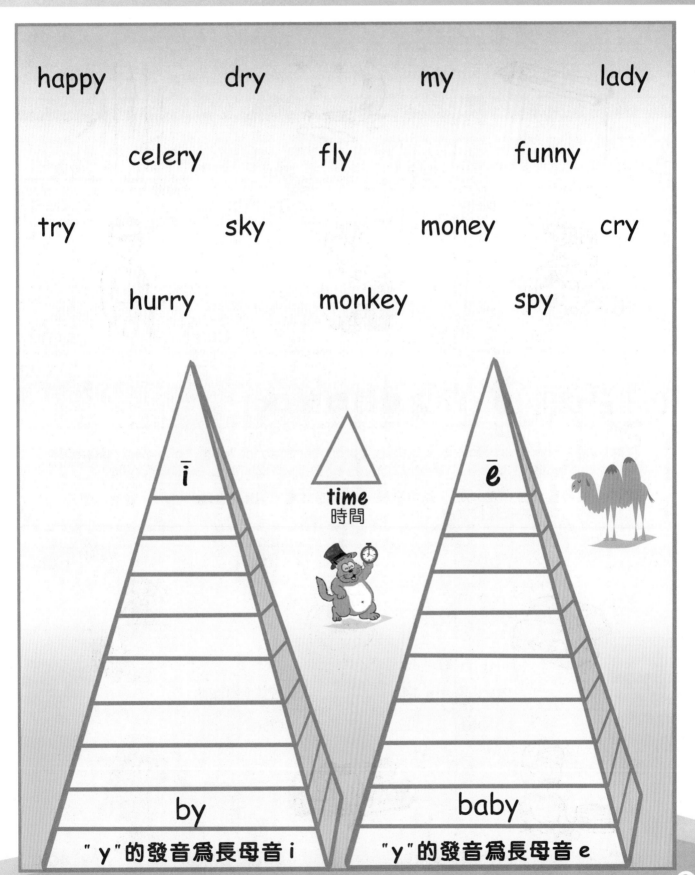

happy   dry   my   lady

celery   fly   funny

try   sky   money   cry

hurry   monkey   spy

$\bar{i}$

time
時間

$\bar{e}$

by

baby

" y " 的發音為長母音 i

" y " 的發音為長母音 e

3

Ii BEFORE GH AND ND (GH 和 ND 之前的母音 Ii)

flight	night	light
light / night	bright / fight	right / might
blind	grind	hind
kind / find	bind / kind	mind / blind

Oo BEFORE LD (Ld 之前的母音 Oo)

gold	fold	hold
old / bold	mold / cold	told / scold
fold	scold	old
mold / told	sold / cold	bold / gold

DIGRAPH LONG OO (複合 OO 長母音) (o͞o) [u]

Definition: **Digraphs** are when two letters are put together to represent a new sound.

定義：當兩個字母在一起只讀作一音時，稱之為複合音。

Directions: Listen and say the picture's name and then circle the pictures that have the **long** " **oo** " sound (example: **z_oo_**).

說明：注意聽並說出圖片的名稱，將含有 **oo** 長音的圖片圈起來。

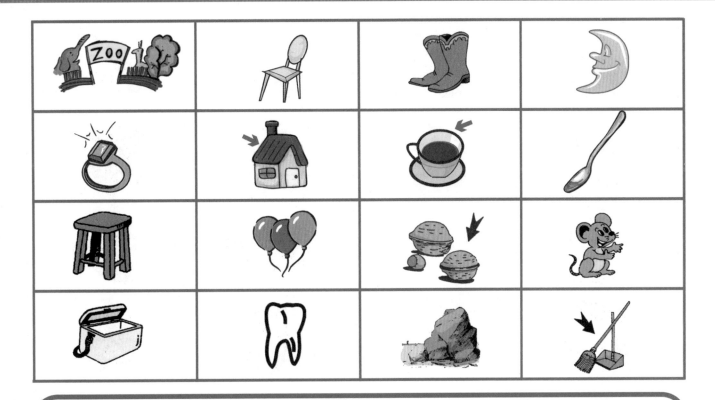

Directions: Listen and say the picture's name and then circle the correct word.

說明：注意聽並說出圖片的名稱，將正確的字圈起來。

noon / moon / moo	spool / pool / stool	roof / rose / root	boom / boots / broom
boat / boost / broom	spoon / stool / soothe	teeth / tooth / toad	zoo / fool / too
pool / balloons / moon	hoop / hope / goose	cooler / tool / tooth	spool / broom / pool

DIGRAPH SHORT OO (複合 OO 短母音) (oo) [U]

Directions: Listen and say the picture's name and then circle the pictures that have the **short " oo "** sound (example: b**oo**k).

說明：注意聽並說出圖片的名稱，將含有 **oo** 短音的圖片圈起來。

Directions: Listen and say the picture's name and then circle the correct word.

說明：注意聽並說出圖片的名稱，將正確的字圈起來。

wood	tooth	brush	woods
cook hood	take took	brook foot	pool root
zoo	book	hood	noon
moon too	hoof brook	goose tool	broom foot
boot	booth	look	hoop
hook book	book pool	soon took	tooth cookies

Directions : Au and aw are <u>usually</u> pronounced as the same sound (examples: **saucer and draw**). Listen and say the picture's name and then circle the pictures that have the " au " or " aw "sound.

說明：Au 和 **aw** 的發音通常相同 **(例如：saucer 和 draw)**。注意聽並說出圖片名稱，將含有 **au** 或 **aw** 的圖片圈起來。

Directions: Listen and say the picture's name and then circle the correct word.
說明：注意聽並說出圖片的名稱，將正確的字圈起來。

straw sauce　　saucer	saw paw　　law	draw claw　　clam	yawn yo-yo　　yell
jaw paw　　saw	faucet caught　　crawl	draw straw　　pawn	raw jaw　　flaw
naughty saucer　daughter	sausage sauce　　mess	law shawl　　draw	straw awning　　crawl

DIGRAPH EA (複合母音 EA) (e) [ε]

Directions: Listen and say the picture's name and then circle the pictures that have the " ea " sound (example: br**ea**d).

說明：注意聽並說出圖片的名稱，將含有 "**ea**" 短音的圖片圈起來。

Directions: Listen and say the picture's name and then circle the correct word.

說明：注意聽並說出圖片的名稱，將正確的字圈起來。

head	saw	swear	bed
fed bear	say paw	sweater sweet	beak bread
feather	thread	met	brat
leather father	head tree	web bean	boat breakfast
peas	thread	bread	sweet
bad net	threat teeth	leather feather	sweat thread

8

DIGRAPH AL（複合母音 AL）

(ô) [ɔ]

Directions: Al is <u>usually</u> pronounced as the " au " or " aw " sound. Listen and say the picture's name and then circle the correct word (example: ba**ll**).

說明：**Al** 的發音通常和 **"au "** 或 **" aw "** 一樣。注意聽並說出圖片的名稱，將正確的字圈起來。

hall	tall	wall
wall　　　ball	small　　　stall	all　　　mall
chalk	talk	walk
salt　　　walk	halt　　　walk	chalk　　　halt

DIGRAPH EW（複合母音 EW）

(ōō) [u]

Directions: Ew is <u>usually</u> pronounced as the long " oo " sound (example: scr**ew**). Listen and say the picture's name ans then circle the correct word.

說明：**Ew** 的發通常跟 **"oo "** 長音一樣 (例如：scr**ew**)。注意聽並說出圖片的名稱，將正確的字圈起來。

crew	fly	blew
slew　　　screw	flew　　　slew	drew　　　boom
grew	cool	blue
goose　　　fool	crew　　　chew	boost　　　brew

9

DIGRAPH CH (複合子音 CH) (ch) [tʃ]

Directions: Listen and say the picture's name. If the name has the " ch " sound,
write ch in the box (example: <u>ch</u>eese).

說明： 注意聽並說出圖片的名稱，如果這名稱含有 " ch " 音，就把 ch 寫在格子內。

Directions: Listen and say the picture's name and then circle the correct word.

說明： 注意聽並說出圖片的名稱，將正確的字圈起來。

chip	cheer	chin	chopsticks
chair crush	chain chest	chip club	check chick
match	check	pitch	children
witch church	reach chick	chimney cheer	chin chain
cheese	peach	batch	choose
chest cheer	crutch chain	branch bench	children chicken

DIGRAPH SH (複合子音 SH)

(sh) [ʃ]

Directions: Listen and say the picture's name. If the name has the " sh " sound, write **sh** in the box (example: <u>sh</u>ark).

說明：注意聽並說出圖片的名稱，如果這名稱含有 "**sh**"音，就把 **sh** 寫在格子內。

Directions: Listen and say the picture's name and then circle the correct word.

說明：注意聽並說出圖片的名稱，將正確的字圈起來。

shower	brush	shade	fish
shirt shorts	spear blush	ship sheep	brush wish
sheep	shark	sleet	shade
shirt sheet	shoulder shower	shopkeeper she	skip shave
shells	sneak	boulder	shrimp
smell small	sleep sheep	shrimp shoulder	fish shot

DIGRAPH VOICELESS TH (複合無聲子音 TH) (th) [θ]

Directions: Voiceless " th " is pronounced as in **three**. Listen and say the picture name and then circle the correct word.

說明：無聲 th 的發音和 **three** 的 th 一樣。注意聽並說出圖片的名稱，將正確的字圈起來。

Note: The " th " sound is pronounced by putting your tongue between your teeth.

注意： 在發無聲 th 音時，要把舌尖輕輕的伸出放置於上下牙齒之間，且**不**震動聲帶。

thirsty	thumb	throw
tooth three	thin wreath	thread thirty
bath	throw	bath
path think	tooth thirteen	wreath path

DIGRAPH VOICED TH (複合有聲子音 TH) (th) [ð]

Directions: Voiced " th " is pronounced as in **mother**. Listen and say the picture name and then circle the correct word.

說明：有聲 th 的發音和 **mother** 的 th 一樣。注意聽並說出圖片的名稱，將正確的字圈起來。

Note: The " th " sound is pronounced by putting your tongue between your teeth.

注意： 在發有聲 th 音時，要把舌尖輕輕的伸出放置於上下牙齒之間，且**要**震動聲帶。

mother	they	them
brother father	leather feather	these this
those	father	the
that the	feather smooth	weather soothe

DIGRAPH WH (複合子音 WH) (hw) [hw]

Directions: Listen and say the picture's name. If the name has the " wh " sound, write **wh** in the box (**example:** <u>wh</u>ale).

說明：注意聽並說出圖片的名稱，如果這名稱含有 "**wh**" 音，就把 **wh** 寫在格子內。

Directions: Listen and say the picture's name and then circle the correct word.

說明：注意聽並說出圖片的名稱，將正確的字圈起來。

which / whiskey / wheat	church / chest / check ✓	whiz / whale / whether	whirl / wheel / wheat
shook / ship / sheep	whiskers / whale / white	whip / which / whiz	thin / thirsty / thirty
weather / whistle / when	whisper / whirl / whip	thumb / three / thread	wish / whisk / whiskey

13

DIGRAPH GH AND PH (複合子音 GH 和 PH) (f) [f]

Directions: Gh and ph are <u>usually</u> pronounced as the " f " sound (**examples: laugh and** **phone**). Listen and say the picture's name and then circle the correct word.

說明： Gh 和 ph 的發音通常和 **"f"** 的發音一樣(**例如：laugh 和 phone**)。注意聽並說出圖片的名稱，將正確的字圈起來。

laugh	enough	cough
tough rough	tough cough	enough laugh
phone	trophy	phonics
phonics photo	graph phone	photo trophy

PYRAMID LISTENING TEST (金字塔辨音測驗)

Directions: Listen and <u>repeat</u> the sound and then circle the correct answer.

說明： 注意聽並跟著唸出這個音，再將正確的答案圈起來。

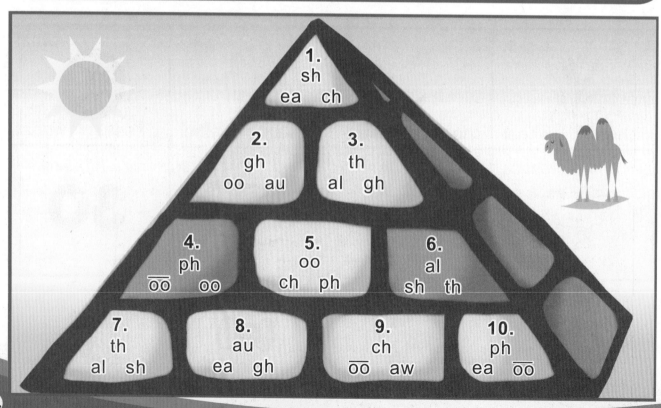

1.
sh
ea   ch

2.
gh
oo   au

3.
th
al   gh

4.
ph
oo   oo

5.
oo
ch   ph

6.
al
sh   th

7.
th
al   sh

8.
au
ea   gh

9.
ch
oo   aw

10.
ph
ea   oo

AN AND AM SOUNDS (AN 和 AM 音)

Directions: Listen and say the picture's name. If the name has the "**an**" sound, write **an** in the box (example: c**an**).

說明： 注意聽並說出圖片的名稱，如果這名稱含有 "**an**" 音，就把 **an** 寫在格子內。

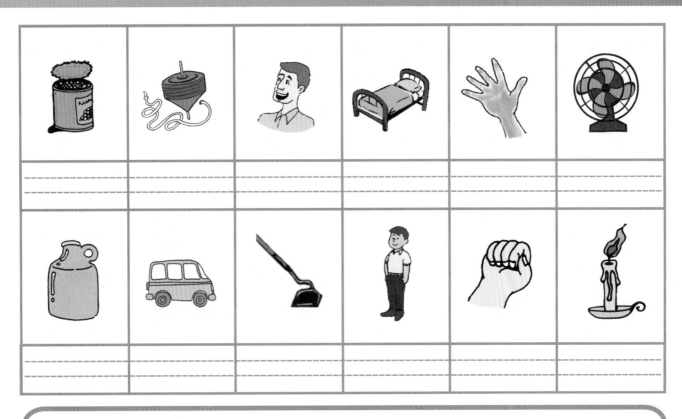

Directions: Listen and say the picture's name. If the name has the "**am**" sound, write **am** in the box (example: h**am**).

說明： 注意聽並說出圖片的名稱，如果這名稱含有 "**am**"，就把 **am** 寫在格子內。

AR SOUND (AR 音)

Directions: Listen and say the picture's name. If the name has the " **ar** " sound,
write **ar** in the box (**example: d<u>ar</u>t**).

說明：注意聽並說出圖片的名稱，如果這名稱含有 **" ar "** 音，就把 **ar** 寫在格子內。

Directions: Listen and say the picture's name and then circle the correct word.

說明：注意聽並說出圖片的名稱，將正確的字圈起來。

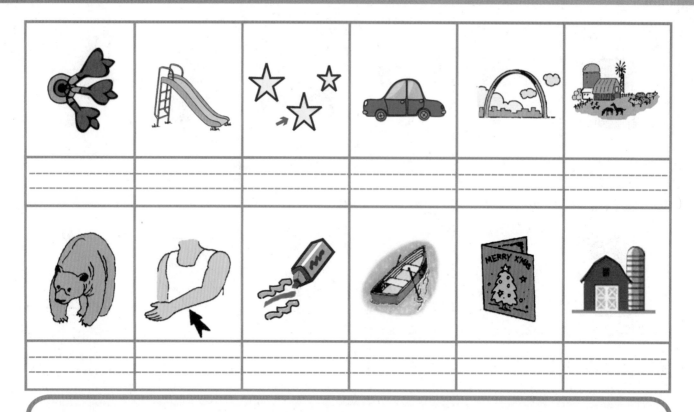

	star		cart		dare		farm
start	stand	scar	card	dam	desk	barn	lark
	yawn		garden		star		can
yarn	yard	pardon	harden	farm	arm	cab	bird
	art		yard		fan		hard
stamp	cake	yawn	yarn	fast	bat	hide	harp

16

OR SOUND (OR音)

Directions: Listen and say the picture's name. If the name has the " **or** " sound, write **or** in the box (example: h<u>or</u>se).

說明：注意聽並說出圖片的名稱，如果這名稱含有 "**or**" 音，就把 **or** 寫在格子內。

_____	_____	_____	_____	_____	_____
_____	_____	_____	_____	_____	_____

Directions: Listen and say the picture's name and then circle the correct word.

說明：注意聽並說出圖片的名稱，將正確的字圈起來。

fog ... cab ...	horse ... march ...
for ... fork ... cane ... corn	hose ... hard ... porch ... torch
orange ... door ...	bore ... floor ...
cord ... organ ... fare ... dare	score ... scare ... forty ... flag
fork ... horn ...	stork ... store ...
card ... cork ... harm ... horse	shorts ... star ... more ... stare

Directions: Listen and say the picture's name. If the name has the " er " sound, write er in the box (example: h**er**d).

說明：注意聽並說出圖片的名稱，如果這名稱含有" er "音，就把 er 寫在格子內。

Directions: Listen and say the picture's name. If the name has the " ir " sound, write **ir** in the box (example: b**ir**d).

說明：注意聽並說出圖片的名稱，如果這名稱含有" ir "音，就把 **ir** 寫在格子內。

UR SOUND (UR 音)

Directions: Listen and say the picture's name. If the name has the " **ur** " sound, write **ur** in the box (example: n**ur**se).

說明：注意聽並說出圖片的名稱，如果這名稱含有 " **ur** " 音，就把 **ur** 寫在格子內。

UNSTRESSED AR ER OR SOUNDS (非重音節之 AR ER OR) (ər) [ə]

Directions: When **ar, er,** and **or** are at the end of a word and <u>not stressed</u>, they are <u>usually</u> pronounced as in **doll<u>ar</u>**, **teach<u>er</u>,** and **doct<u>or</u>**. Listen and say the picture's name and then circle the correct word.

說明：當 ar、er、和 or 在一個字的字尾且不為重音之所在，他們的發音和 **doll<u>ar</u>** 的 ar，**teach<u>er</u>** 的 er 以及 **doct<u>or</u>** 的 or 一樣。注意聽並說出圖片的名稱，將正確的字圈起來。

sugar	sneakers	doctor
solar dollar	teacher marker	editor tractor
calendar	ruler	vendor
collar solar	eraser spider	sailor mirror

19

ER IR UR PRACTICE (ER IR UR 練習)

Directions: Listen and say the picture's name and then circle the correct word.

說明：注意聽並說出圖片的名稱，將正確的字圈起來。

start score	pine port	herd hard
shirt skirt	porch purse	help ham
square sport	number name	bean bird
spark squirrel	nose nurse	barn burn
skirt score	far farm	turnip turtle
shirt shorts	turn fern	turkey termite
chicken car	tart dirt	mermaid march
church chore	turn thirty	man murmur
target termites	camp cure	shark stir
turkey thirty	curb card	sit spark
girl garden	run ruler	thirteen thirsty
gale ginger	racket rain	turkey turn

20

DIPHTHONGS OI AND OY (雙母音 OI 和 OY) (oi) [ɔɪ]

Directions: **Diphthongs** are two vowel sounds pronounced together making one sound.

定義：當兩個母音一起發音成為一組母音，稱之為**雙母音**。

Directions: **Oi** and **oy** are <u>usually</u> pronounced as the same sound (**examples:** <u>oil</u> and <u>boy</u>). Listen and say the picture's name and then circle the pictures that have the "**oi**" or "**oy**" sound.

說明： **Oi** 和 **oy** 的發音通常相同 (例如：<u>oil</u> 和 <u>boy</u>)。注意聽並說出圖片的名稱，將含有 " **oi** " 和 " **oy** " 音的圖片圈起來。

Directions: Listen and say the picture's name and then circle the correct word.

說明：注意聽並說出圖片的名稱，將正確的字圈起來。

toilet  coy toys	boy bay joy	coin coil foil	loyal coil boil
troy joint toilet	toy soil coin	noise enjoy moist	foil soil destroy
hoist point joint	oil spoil coil	pet point poison	joint join jam

21

DIPHTHONGS OU AND OW (雙母音 OU 和 OW) (ou) [aʊ]

Directions: **Ou** and **ow** are <u>usually</u> pronounced as the same sound (examples: h<u>ou</u>se and <u>ow</u>l). Listen and say the picture's name and then circle the pictures that have the " **ou** " or " **ow** " sound.

說明：Ou 和 **ow** 的發音通常相同 (例如：h<u>ou</u>se 和 <u>ow</u>l)。注意聽並說出圖片的名稱，將含有 **ou** 和 **ow** 音的圖片圈起來。

Directions: Listen and say the picture's name and then circle the correct word.

說明：注意聽並說出圖片的名稱，將正確的字圈起來。

prowl	clown	blouse	moo
clown vowels	crown cloud	foul loud	mouse house
flower	hound	owl	scowl
sour snout	scout house	towel blouse	shout snout
sound	mouth	prowl	hound
shower round	south pouch	cloud clown	sour owl

OW SOUND PYRAMID PRACTICE (OW 音金字塔練習)

Directions: When ow is in the middle of a word or a syllable, it is <u>usually</u> pronounced as the " **ou** " sound (example: <u>dow</u>n). When ow is at the end of a word or a syllable, it is <u>usually</u> pronounced as the **long** " **o** " sound (example: <u>slow</u>). Listen and write the words with the long " **o** " sound in the left pyramid and the ones with the " **ou** " sound in the right pyramid.

說明： 當 ow 出現在一個字或音節之中時，它通常會發成 ou 的發音 (例如：<u>dow</u>n)。而當 ow 出現在一個字或音節之尾時，它通常會發成長母音 " o " 的發音 (例如：<u>slow</u>)。注意聽下列的字，將 ow 發長母音 o 的字填入左的金字塔中，而 ow 發 ou 音的字則填入右邊的金字塔內。

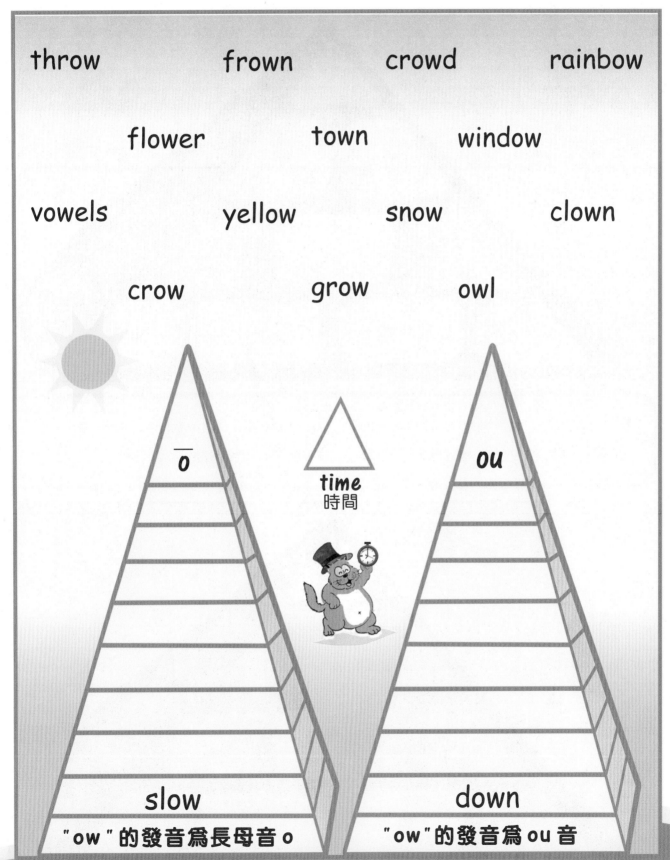

throw   frown   crowd   rainbow

flower   town   window

vowels   yellow   snow   clown

crow   grow   owl

ō

ou

time
時間

slow

down

" ow " 的發音為長母音 o

" ow " 的發音為 ou 音

PYRAMID LISTENING TEST (金字塔辨音測驗)

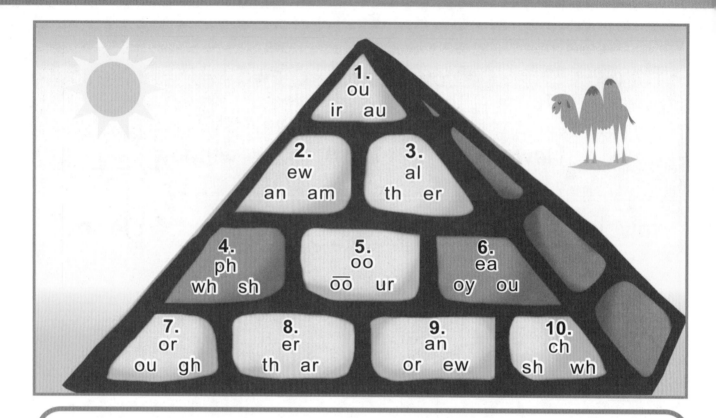

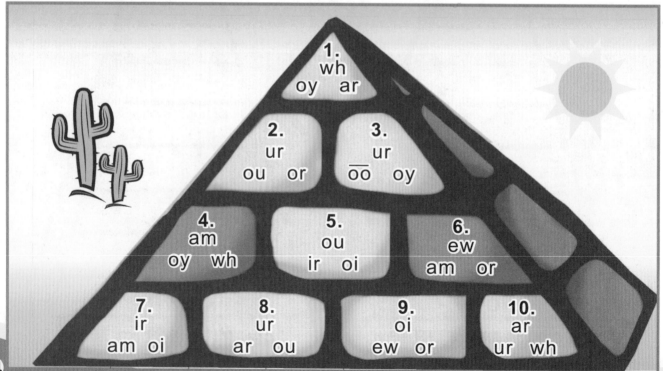

24

KN SOUND（KN 音）

knew know	knit knife	know knew
knob knit	knack knelt	knee knead
knuckle knelt	knelt knee	knit knot
knoll knack	knew knock	knife knelt

WR SOUND （WR 音）

wreck wrestle	wrench wrap	wreck wrack
wrath wreath	wrack wrist	wrench wreath
write writ	wrist wrath	write wrench
right wrote	wrinkles wrestle	wrap wrist

GHT SOUND (GHT 音)

Directions: Although **gh** is <u>usually</u> pronounced as the " **f** " sound, **gh** is silent when followed by **t** (**example: eight**). Listen and say the picture's name and then circle the correct word.

說明： 雖然 **gh** 的發音通常和 **f** 的發音一樣，但 **gh** 後面跟隨著 **t** 時，**gh** 通常就不發音（例如：ei**ght**）。注意聽並說出圖片的名稱，將正確的字圈起來。

caught	daughter	flight
night — eight	bought — taught	bought — daughter
straight	fight	night
right — flight	straight — eight	right — caught

MB SOUND (MB 音)

Directions: When **m** and **b** are together, **b** is <u>usually</u> silent. Only the " **m** " sound is pronounced (**example: comb**). Listen and say the picture's name and then circle the correct word.

說明： 當 **m** 和 **b** 在一起時，**b** 通常不發音，只有發 **m** 的音。注意聽並說出圖片的名稱再圈出正確的字。

comb	climb	thumb
bomb — lamb	tomb — thumb	bomb — comb
climb	tomb	thumb
tomb — lamb	comb — bomb	climb — lamb

TCH SOUND（TCH 音）

> **Directions:** In **tch** spellings, **t** is <u>usually</u> silent. Only the " **ch** " sound is pronounced (**example: wa<u>tch</u>**). Listen and say the picture's name and then circle the correct word.
>
> **說明**：當 **tch** 在一起時，**t** 通常不發音，只發 **ch** 的音（例如：**wa<u>tch</u>**）。注意聽並說出圖片的名稱，將正確的字圈起來。

watch	catch	match
batch kitchen	switch witch	crutch pitcher
catch	switch	batch
watch kitchen	witch crutch	pitcher watch

FINAL GE SOUND（字尾 GE 音）　　　　　（j）[dʒ]

> **Directions:** When **g** and **e** are together, **ge** is <u>usually</u> pronounced as the " **j** " sound (**example: bad<u>ge</u>**). Listen and say the picture's name and then circle the correct word.
>
> **說明**：當 **g** 和 **e** 在一起時，**ge** 的發音通常跟 **j** 的發音一樣（例如：**bad<u>ge</u>**）。注意聽並說出圖片的名稱，將正確的字圈起來。

vegetable	stage	age
bandage badge	edge page	orange strange
germ	wage	stage
pledge bridge	gem wedge	range general

Directions: Listen and say the picture's name. If the name ends the " le " sound, write **le** in the box (example: app**le**).

說明： 注意聽並說出圖片的名稱，如果這名稱是以 **le** 音為結尾，就把 **le** 寫在格子內。

Directions: Listen and say the picture's name and then circle the correct word.

說明： 注意聽並說出圖片的名稱，將正確的字圈起來。

tile	kettle	apple	knuckle
turtle　　table	buckle　　marble	candle　　beagle	freckle　　gamble
table	puzzle	handle	mail
triangle　bubbles	noodle　　needle	steeple　　turtle	noodles　　needle
marble	people	whistle	candle
needle vegetables	eagle　　apple	whale　　pickle	beetle　　little

28

NG AND NK SOUND (NG 和 NK 音)　　([ŋ]) ([ŋk])

> **Directions:** When **ng** and **nk** are at the end of a word or a syllable, " **ng** " is usually pronounced as in **sing** (the g is silent), and " **nk** " is pronounced as in **think** (the k is pronounced). Listen and say the picture's name and then circle the correct word.
>
> **說明：** 當 **ng** 和 **nk** 在一個字或音節之尾時，通常 **ng** 的發音就如同 **sing** 的 ng 一樣（ **g** 不發音），而 **nk** 的發音就如同 **think** 的 nk 一樣（ **k** 有發音）。注意聽並說出圖片的名稱，將正確的字圈起來。

bring	ring	string
sing　　swing	awning　　king	strong　　spring
thank	pink	ink
drink　　think	bank　　tank	stink　　think

ISION USION SURE SOUNDS (ISION USION SURE 音)　(zh) [ʒ]

> **Directions:** Listen and say the picture's name and then circle the correct word (**examples: tele*vis*ion, con*fus*ion, and trea*sure***).
>
> **說明：** 注意聽並說出圖片的名稱，將正確的字圈起來。

supervision	collision	division
television　　decision	vision　　television	collision　　confusion
leisure	measure	leisure
measure　　treasure	pleasure　　leisure	pleasure　　treasure

TION SOUND (TION 音)

Directions: Listen and say the picture's name and then circle the correct word (**example: sta<u>tion</u>**).

說明：注意聽並說出圖片的名稱，將正確的字圈起來。

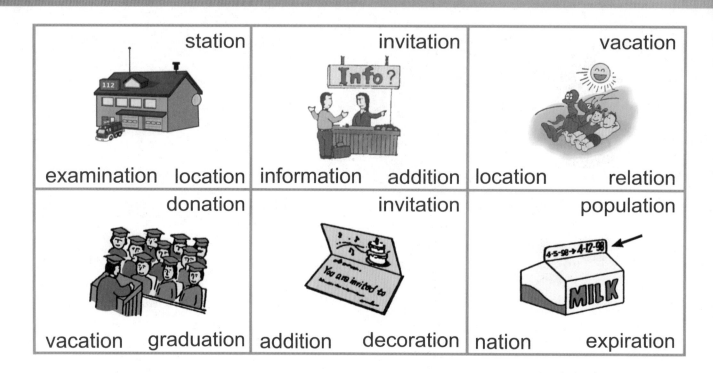

station	invitation	vacation
examination location	information addition	location relation
donation	invitation	population
vacation graduation	addition decoration	nation expiration

TURE SOUND (TURE 音)

Directions: Listen and say the picture's name and then circle the correct word (**example: pic<u>ture</u>**).

說明：注意聽並說出圖片的名稱，將正確的字圈起來。

pasture	picture	signature
picture legislature	nature acupuncture	caricature mature
temperature	mature	furniture
pasture signature	adventure nature	literature mixture

BLENDS: BL CL FL (混合音：BL CL FL)

Definition: When two or three consonant sounds are together, they are called <u>blends</u>.

定義：當兩個或三個子音在一起發音時，它們就是所謂的**混合音**。

Directions: Listen and say the picture's name. If the name has the "**bl**", "**cl**", or "**fl**" sound, write **bl**, **cl**, or **fl** in the box (**examples: <u>bl</u>ouse, <u>cl</u>own, and <u>fl</u>ute**).

說明：注意聽並說出圖片的名稱，如果這名稱含有"**bl**"、"**cl**"或"**fl**"的音，就把 **bl**、**cl** 或 **fl** 寫在格子內。

_____	_____	_____	_____	_____	_____
_____	_____	_____	_____	_____	_____

Directions: Listen and say the picture's name and then circle the correct word.

說明：注意聽並說出圖片的名稱，將正確的字圈起來。

flow flower floor	blocks blue black	clouds climb clean	flat fly flag
class clap clock	close clown claw	flood fly flame	blond blank blackboard
blond blew blouse	flash flood floor	blade blank blond	claw cliff clap

BLENDS: GL PL SL (混合音：GL PL SL)

Directions: Listen and say the picture's name. If the name has the "gl", "pl" or "sl" sound, write **gl**, **pl**, or **sl** in the box (examples: **glue, plug, and sleep**).

說明：注意聽並說出圖片的名稱，如果這名稱含有 **"gl"**、**"pl"** 或 **"sl"** 的音，就把 **gl**、**pl** 或 **sl** 寫在格子內。

Directions: Listen and say the picture's name and then circle the correct word.

說明：注意聽並說出圖片的名稱，將正確的字圈起來。

glaze · glad · globe	slot · sled · slip	glider · globe · glass	plant · plate · planet
sleigh · slide · slice	play · plank · plant	sleep · slave · sleeve	plan · plums · plus
plug · plum · pan	glass · glaze · glance	glad · glue · glider	sleeve · slip · sleep

BLENDS: BR CR DR (混合音：BR CR DR)

Directions: Listen and say the picture's name. If the name has the " br ", " cr ", or " dr " sound, write **br**, **cr**, or **dr** in the box (examples: <u>br</u>ead, <u>cr</u>ab, and <u>dr</u>um).

說明： 注意聽並說出圖片的名稱，如果這名稱含有 **" br "**、**" cr "** 或 **" dr "** 的音，就把 **br** 、 **cr** 或 **dr** 寫在格子內。

Directions: Listen and say the picture's name and then circle the correct word.

說明： 注意聽並說出圖片的名稱，將正確的字圈起來。

broom	drip	crew	drip
breakfast brother	drive drink	crow cream	drop dream
crash	dragon	bring	cross
crazy crane	drum drive	bride braid	drip cream
dry	bridge	crack	broke
drive dress	branch brake	crab crawl	bread brat

BLENDS: FR GR （混合音：FR GR）

Directions: Listen and say the picture's name. If the name has the " fr " or " gr " sound, write **fr** or **gr** in the box (examples: <u>fr</u>og and <u>gr</u>apes).

說明： 注意聽並說出圖片的名稱，如果這名稱含有 " fr " 或 " gr " 的音，就把 fr 或 gr 寫在格子內。

Directions: Listen and say the picture's name and then circle the correct word.

說明： 注意聽並說出圖片的名稱，將正確的字圈起來。

free / front / frog	grill / grin / grid	fruit / frown / front	grass / graze / grade
fret / fry / fruit	gray / grasp / graph	grade / grip / gripe	freckle / fresh / freezer
grow / grapes / grew	frown / freckles / frighten	friend / from / frame	grass / green / greet

BLENDS: PR TR （混合音：PR TR）

Directions: Listen and say the picture's name. If the name has the " **pr** " or " **tr** " sound, write **pr** or **tr** in the box (examples: <u>pr</u>esent and <u>tr</u>ee).

說明： 注意聽並說出圖片的名稱，如果這名稱含有 " **pr** " 或 " **tr** " 的音，就把 **pr** 或 **tr** 寫在格子內。

Directions: Listen and say the picture's name and then circle the correct word.

說明： 注意聽並說出圖片的名稱，將正確的字圈起來。

trip triangle tripod	pray prize present	tree truck trade	trap trash train
price praise prank	trail trophy tramp	pretty pretzel print	prison prince prisoner
track trunk tractor	trap tree truck	pray preach price	practice princess prince

BLENDS: SK SM SN SP (混合音：SK SM SN SP)

Directions: Listen and say the picture's name. If the name has the "**sk**", "**sm**", "**sn**" or "**sp**" sound, write **sk**, **sm**, **sn** or **sp** in the box (examples: <u>sk</u>ate, <u>sm</u>oke, <u>sn</u>eakers, and <u>sp</u>oon).

說明：注意聽並說出圖片的名稱，如果這名稱含有"**sk**"、"**sm**"、"**sn**"或"**sp**"的音，就把**sk**、**sm**、**sn**或**sp**寫在格子內。

Directions: Listen and say the picture's name and then circle the correct word.

說明：注意聽並說出圖片的名稱，將正確的字圈起來。

snack / snail / sneakers	spoon / spin / spaghetti	skill / skirt / skit	smoke / smell / small
scar / spoon / scan	snore / snake / snowman	small / smirk / smog	skip / skirt / skates
smile / smart / smooth	skull / sketch / skunk	snake / snack / snow	scarf / spider / scar

36

BLENDS: SC ST SW (混合音：SC ST SW)

sweet	splash	stand	sweep
sweater sweat	speak score	stone stove	small switch
stay	swam	scale	store
stop stars	swing swim	spice spoon	stand stamp
scarf	student	swim	spar
spider spin	stairs stamp	swing sweater	school spare

37

BLENDS: SCR SPL SPR SQU STR (混合音：SCR SPL SPR SQU STR)

Directions: Listen and say the picture's name. If the name has the " scr ", " spl ", " spr", " squ ", or " str " sound, write the correct blend in in the box (examples: <u>scr</u>ew, <u>spl</u>it, <u>spr</u>ay, <u>squ</u>are, and <u>str</u>aw).

說明：注意聽並說出圖片的名稱，如果這名稱含有 " scr " 、 " spl " 、 " spr " 、 " squ " 或 " str " 音，就把 scr 、 spl 、 spr 、 squ 或 str 寫在格子內。

Directions: Listen and say the picture's name and then circle the correct word.

說明：注意聽並說出圖片的名稱，將正確的字圈起來。

straw	spread	scrub	sprout
strand stream	spray spring	scrape screw	sprain sprint
squeak	strain	splash	straw
squirrel squirt	strong string	spleen split	strawberry strip
split	scratch	stripes	squeak
splash spleen	screen scream	straight stroke	squirt square

38

SUFFIXES: ES IES VES S (字尾變化：ES IES VES S)

Rule 1: If a word ends in **ch, sh, s, x,** or **z,** we <u>usually</u> add " **es** " to form the plural (examples : wa<u>tches</u>, bru<u>shes</u>, bu<u>ses</u>, bo<u>xes</u>, or bu<u>zzes</u>).

規則1：一個字的字尾為 **ch, sh, s, x,** 或 **z** 時，通常加 " **es** " 來形成複數形 (例如：wa<u>tches</u>、 bru<u>shes</u>、 bu<u>ses</u>、 bo<u>xes</u> 或 bu<u>zzes</u>)。

Rule 2: If a word ends in **y** <u>after</u> a consonant, we <u>usually</u> change the **y** to **i** and then add " **es** " (examples: fl<u>y</u> - fl<u>ies</u>, baby - bab<u>ies</u>).

規則2：字尾為子音+ **y** 時，去 **y** 再加 " **ies** " (例如：fl<u>y</u> - fl<u>ies</u>、 bab<u>y</u> - bab<u>ies</u>)。

Rule 3: If a word ends in **f** or **fe,** we <u>usually</u> drop the **f** or **fe** first and then add " **ves** " (example: knife - kni<u>ves</u>).

規則3：字尾為子音 **f** 或 **fe** 時，通常去 **f** 或 **fe** 再加 **" ves "** (例如：knife-knives)。

Rule 4: Otherwise, we <u>usually</u> just add " **s** " after a root word (examples: dog - dogs, pen - pens).

規則4：其他的變化通常只要加上 **s** 即可。

Directions: Write and then say the following words in their correct forms.

說明：寫出並說出下列字的正確形式。

Rule 1 規則1		Rules 2 and3 規則2和3		Rule 4 規則4	
bus		knife		dog	
fox		wife		rake	
church		loaf		can	
brush		berry		whale	
glass		copy		bear	
match		leaf		apple	
dress		city		girl	
bench		fly		saucer	
buzz		life		bat	

SUFFIXES: ES IES VES S TEST (ES IES VES S 字尾變化測驗)

Directions: Listen and make the following words **plural** and then put them in the correct pyramid.

說明：注意聽下列的字，寫出它們的**複數形**，再將它們填入正確的金字塔中。

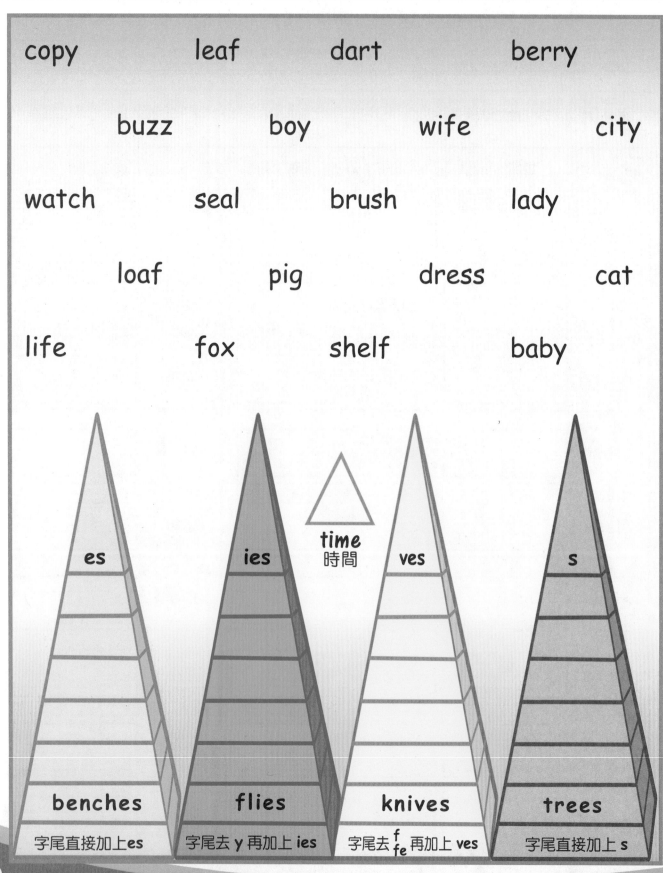

copy   leaf   dart   berry

buzz   boy   wife   city

watch   seal   brush   lady

loaf   pig   dress   cat

life   fox   shelf   baby

es   ies   **time** 時間   ves   s

benches   flies   knives   trees

字尾直接加上es   字尾去 y 再加上 ies   字尾去 f fe 再加上 ves   字尾直接加上 s

SUFFIXES: ED AND IED (字尾變化：ED 和 IED)

Rule 1: If **ed** is added to a word ending in **d** or **t**, it is <u>usually</u> pronounced as the " **id** " sound (examples: **needed** or **wanted**).

規則1：字的結尾為 **d** 或 **t** 時，加上 **ed** 之後，**ed** 的發音就配合前面的子音 **d** 或 **t**，發成 " **did** " 或 " **tid** " 音 (例如：**needed** 或 **wanted**)。

Rule 2: If **ed** is added to a <u>voiced</u> word ending, it is <u>usually</u> pronounced as the " **d** " sound (example: **played**).

規則2：字的結尾為有聲音時，**ed** 就發 **d** 音 (例如：**played**)。

Rule 3: If **ed** is added to a <u>voiceless</u> word ending, it is <u>usually</u> pronounced as the " **t** " sound (example: **watched**).

規則3：字的結尾為無聲音時，**ed** 就發 **t** 音 (例如：**watched**)。

Rule 4: If **ed** is added to a word ending in **y** after a consonant, we <u>usually</u> change the **y** to **i** and then add " **ed** ". It is then pronounced as **rule 2** (example: **study-studied**).

規則4：字的字尾為子音+ **y** 時，通常去 **y** 再加上 **ied**，發音如同**規則2** (例如：**study-studied**)。

Directions: Write and then say the following words in their correct " **ed** " forms.

說明：寫出並說出下列的正確形式。

Rule 1 規則1		Rules 2 and3 規則2和3		Rule 4 規則4	
head		cook		copy	
point		play		try	
sound		mail		hurry	
paint		clean		spy	
end		kiss		reply	
wait		close		fry	
land		wash		empty	
count		hope		deny	

SUFFIX ED TEST (ED 字尾變化測驗)

Directions: Listen and make the following words **past tense** and then put them in the correct pyramid.

說明：注意聽下列的字，寫出它們的**過去式**，再將它們填入正確的金字塔中。

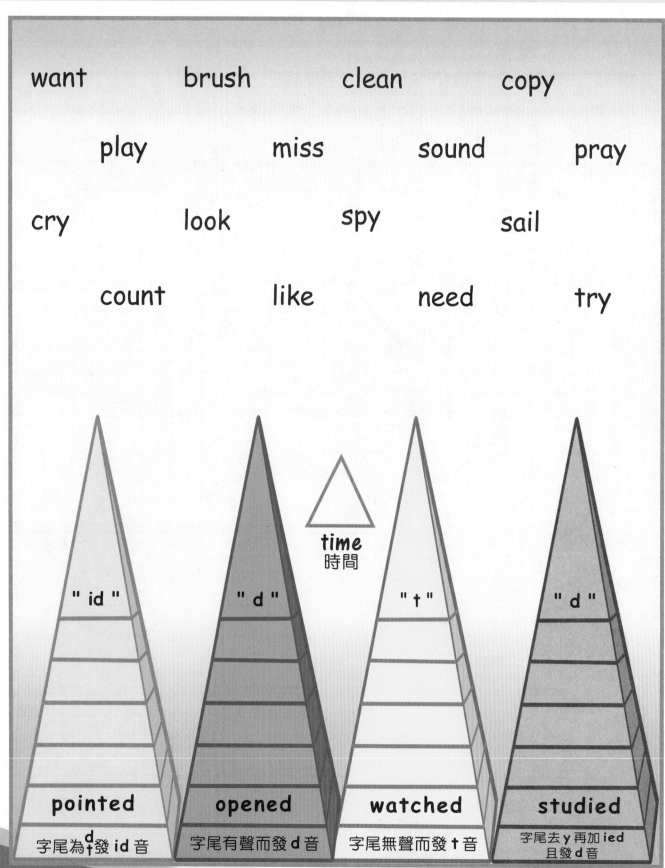

want   brush   clean   copy

play   miss   sound   pray

cry   look   spy   sail

count   like   need   try

time
時間

" id "   " d "   " t "   " d "

pointed   **opened**   **watched**   **studied**

字尾為 d/t 發 id 音   字尾有聲而發 d 音   字尾無聲而發 t 音   字尾去 y 再加 ied 且發 d 音

SUFFIXES: FINAL CONSONANT DOUBLED (字尾變化：字尾子音重複)

Rule: When a word ends in a <u>single</u> consonant, we <u>usually</u> double the consonant before adding "ed" or "ing" (examples: <u>ho</u>pped or <u>ho</u>pping).

規則: 一個字的結尾為短母音＋單一子音時，在加 **ed** 或 **ing** 之前要重複字尾的子音字母 (例如：<u>ho</u>pped 或 <u>ho</u>pping)。

Directions: Write the following words in their correct "ed" and "ing" forms.

說明: 將下列字改成 "**ed**" 和 "**ing**" 的形式。

ed	Root Word 字根	ing
	hop	
	jog	
	pet	
	map	
	hug	
	knit	
	beg	
	stop	
	hum	
	shop	

SUFFIXES AFTER SILENT E (無聲 E 之後的字尾變化)

Rule: When adding "**ed**" or "**ing**" after a word ending with a silent e, we <u>usually</u> drop the e first and then add "**ed**" or "**ing**" (examples: bak<u>ed</u> or bak<u>ing</u>).

規則：一個字的結尾為不發音的 e 時，通常先去掉 e 再加上 **ed** 或 **ing**（例如：bak**ed** 或 bak**ing**）。

Directions: Write the following words in their correct "**ed**" and "**ing**" forms.

說明：將下列字改成"**ed**"和"**ing**"的形式。

ed	Root Word 字根	ing
	bake	
	use	
	shave	
	skate	
	rake	
	close	
	site	
	dance	
	raise	
	grade	

CONTRACTIONS (縮寫式)

Definition: **Contractions** are the making of two words into one word without changing the meaning **(example: I am = I'm)**.

定義： 將兩個字寫成一個字的形式，且不改變其原來的字義，稱之為縮寫式。

Directions: In the boxes below, listen and draw a line from left to right to the correct contraction.

說明： 連連看，將左右兩邊的意思相同的字連起來。

I am	you're	we have	I'll
you are	she's	they have	we've
he is	I'm	I will	you'll
she is	he's	you will	they've
it is	I've	he will	it'll
we are	they're	she will	we'll
they are	we're	it will	she'll
I have	it's	we will	he'll
you have	it's	they will	they'll
he has	she's	let us	isn't
she has	you've	are not	let's
it has	he's	is not	aren't
have not	hadn't	will not	don't
has not	haven't	do not	won't
had not	can't	does not	didn't
can not	hasn't	did not	doesn't

CONTRACTIONS TEST （縮寫式測驗）

Directions: Listen and write the **contraction** of each pair of words below. After you've finished, practice saying each contraction.

說明：寫出下列的縮寫式。完成後，練習說出每一個縮寫式。

I am	**I'm**	she is	_____
it is	_____	you are	_____
I have	_____	he has	_____
we have	_____	you have	_____
he will	_____	it will	_____
they will	_____	you will	_____
are not	_____	did not	_____
have not	_____	does not	_____
let us	_____	has not	_____
do not	_____	is not	_____
we will	_____	she will	_____
can not	_____	I will	_____
it has	_____	they have	_____
she has	_____	will not	_____
they are	_____	we are	_____
he is	_____	had not	_____

SYLLABLE(S) (音節)

Syllable: A word or part of a word which contains <u>one vowel sound</u> or consonant acting as a vowel
(**example: yesterday= <u>yes-ter-day</u>).**
音節：一個 " 有聲 " 母音構成一個音節，有幾個母音就有幾個音節（**例如**： yesterday= <u>yes-ter-day</u>）。
Directions: Listen and say the word and then write the number of syllables below it.
說明：注意聽並說出下列的字，將它們的音節數寫在下面的線上。
Note: Vowel **digraphs** and **diphthongs** are read as <u>one syllable</u>. 複合母音和雙母音應視為<u>一個母音</u>。

yesterday **3** ___	student ___	wrinkles ___
dog ___	screwdriver ___	economical ___
shorts ___	international ___	decision ___
doctor ___	eraser ___	witch ___
bicycle ___	robe ___	signature ___
chopsticks ___	blouse ___	church ___
university ___	dresses ___	marker ___
coins ___	responsibility ___	congratulations ___
pronounce ___	important ___	thumb ___
phonics ___	cooler ___	daughter ___
direction ___	orange ___	unfortunately ___

ANTONYMS HOMONYMS SYNONYMS (反義字 同音字 同義字)

Antonyms: Words that have <u>opposite</u> meanings. (反義字)
Homonyms: Words that <u>sound the same</u> but have <u>different</u> meanings. (同音字)
Synonyms: Words that <u>almost</u> have the same meanings. (同義字)
Directions: Listen to the words on the left and draw a line to the correct match.
說明： 注意聽左列的字，連連看，連接其正確的反義字、同音字或同義字。

Antonyms 反義字		Homonyms 同音字		Synonyms 同義字	
yes	small	two	tale	easy	join
big	no	tail	meat	connect	ill
good	bad	meet	to	sick	simple
rich	close	sail	role	big	little
on	off	sea	sale	quick	large
open	poor	roll	see	small	fast
hot	thin	blue	blew	present	gift
clean	cold	knew	hear	blend	pick
fat	dirty	here	new	choose	mix
tall	last	eight	male	ocean	say
first	noisy	mail	bee	middle	sea
quiet	short	be	ate	speak	center
long	frown	sole	heel	quit	auto
strong	short	heal	soul	car	stop
smile	weak	seem	seam	tardy	late

ZUKE'S BAD ADVICE

Note: This story was written with almost all the sounds you have learned using **The Pyramid Method**.

Last week, Zuke the mule caught a cold, so he went to see Zike. Zike likes to fool people. And he told Zuke to sit in a puddle of mud for three days and three nights, and soon his cold might go away.

So Zuke sat in the mud for three days and waited for his cold to go away. After three days, Zuke still had a cold. So he went to see Nox. Nox is a very smart turtle, but he too likes to fool people. And he told Zuke to sit on the roof of an old barn and sing for three days and soon his cold might go away. So Zuke sat on the roof of an old barn and sang until he was so tired that he fell off the roof and landed on Lox.

"What are you doing on the roof?" Lox asked Zuke. "I'm trying to get rid of my cold. First, Zike told me to sit in mud for three days. Next, Nox told me to sit on the roof of an old barn and sing for three days. I don't know what to do." "I know what you can do. A cold lasts for about eight to twelve days. Since it's already been six days, why don't you sit in the mud for three more days and sit on the roof for three more days and then your cold will be gone*!!*

Can you solve the puzzle?
Use all the letters on the back of the book cover.

_____!

被愚弄的祖克

註: 這個故事是以金字塔學習法中所學習到的主題音所編寫而成的 。

上個星期， 一隻名叫祖克的騾子感冒了，他跑去找柴克。然而，柴克總是喜歡捉弄別人。柴克告訴祖克：「想要治好感冒只要在泥沼中坐個三天三夜，那麼感冒就會很快地消失了。」

祖克信以真就在泥沼中坐了三天三夜，期待感冒趕快好起了。但三天之後，祖克還是覺得不舒服，他只好去找那克斯。那克斯是隻非常聰明的烏龜，但他也喜歡捉弄別人，那克斯告訴祖克：「只要坐在一個老穀倉的屋頂上大聲唱歌，唱個三天三夜，那麼很快地感冒就會好起來了。」然後祖克就照著他的話去做；一直唱一直唱，直到他累的從屋頂上滾了下來，落在拉克斯的身上。

拉克斯就問祖克：「你在屋頂上做什麼？」祖克回答：「我只是想趕快地治好我的感冒。首先柴克要我坐泥沼中三天三夜。接著那克斯又要我在老穀倉的屋頂上大唱三天三夜，可是我還是不舒服，我真的不知道該怎麼辦。」拉克斯靈機一動；告訴祖克：「感冒大約要八～十二天才會好。既然你已經過了六天，你何不再坐在泥沼中三天三夜，然後再坐在老穀倉的屋頂上大唱個三天三夜，那麼你的感冒就會消失了*!!*」

您可以用封底的15個字母拼出一個字來嗎？

—————————————————！

Glossary 字彙

Aa

acupuncture (ak'yōō puŋk'chər)　針灸
addition (ə dish'ən)　加；加之
adventure (ad ven'chər)　探險
advice (ad vīs')　建議
ate (āj)　年紀
ago (ə gō')　以前
airplane (er'plān')　飛機
all (ôl)　都；全部
allege (ə lej')　無證據之宣稱
and (and)　和；且
ant (ant)　螞蟻
ape (āp)　猿猴
apple (ap'əl)　蘋果
arch (ärch)　拱門
arm (ärm)　手臂
art (ärt)　藝術
at (at)　在…
ate (āt)　吃 (過去式)
auto (ôt'ō)　汽車
average (av'rij)　平均
　　　　　(av'ər ij)
away (ə wā')　離開；去別處
awning (ôn'jŋ)　雨篷
ax (aks)　斧頭

Bb

baby (bā'bē)　嬰兒
back (bak)　背部；後面
bad (bad)　壞的
badge (baj)　微章
bag (bag)　袋子
bake (bāk)　烘烤
ball (bôl)　球
balloon (bə lōōn')　氣球
ban (ban)　禁止
bandage (ban'dij)　繃帶
bank (baŋk)　銀行
bar (bär)　酒吧；條狀物
barn (bärn)　穀倉
bat (bat)　球棒；蝙蝠
batch (bach)　一批；一組
bath (bath)　洗澡
bay (bā)　海灣
be (bē)　"是"的原形
beagle (bē'gəl)　小獵兔犬 (米格魯犬)
beak (bēk)　鳥嘴
bean (bēn)　豆子
bear (ber)　熊
bed (bed)　床
bee (bē)　蜜蜂

been (ben)　"是" (過去分詞)；去過…
beet (bēt)　甜菜
beetle (bēt' 'l)　甲蟲
beg (beg)　懇求
bell (bel)　鈴；鐘
belt (belt)　皮帶
bench (bench)　長凳
berry (ber'ē)　漿果
bet (bet)　打賭
beverage (bev'rij)　飲料
　　　　　(bev'ər ij)
bib (bib)　圍兜
big (big)　大的
bike (bīk)　單車
bind (bīnd)　捆綁
bird (bʋrd)　鳥
birthday (bʋrth dā')　生日
bit (bit)　一點；一些
bite (bīt)　咬
black (blak)　黑色
blackboard (blak-bôrd')　黑板
blade (blād)　刀口
blank (blaŋk)　空白
blend (blend)　混合
blew (blōō)　吹 (過去式)
blind (blīnd)　瞎的
block (bläk)　積木；阻擋
bland (bländ)　金髮
blouse (blous)　女用襯衫
blow (blō)　吹
blue (blōō)　藍色
blush (blush)　臉紅
boat (bōt)　小舟；船
boil (boil)　煮沸
bold (bōld)　無畏的；粗體字
bomb (bäm)　炸彈
bone (bōn)　骨頭
book (book)　書
boom (bōōm)　繁榮；隆隆作聲
boost (bōōst)　向上推；增加
booth (bōōth)　亭；攤子
boot (bōōt)　長靴
bore (bôr)　令人厭煩
bottle (bät' 'l)　瓶子
bought (bôt)　買 (過去式；過去分詞)
boulder (bōl'dər)　巨石
bowl (bōl)　碗
box (bäks)　盒子
boy (boi)　男孩
braid (brād)　辮子
brake (brāk)　煞車

51

Glossary 字彙

branch (branch) 樹枝
brat (brat) 頑皮傢伙
bread (bred) 麵包
breakfast (brek'fəst) 早餐
brew (brōō) 沖泡
bride (brīd) 新娘
bridge (brij) 橋
bright (brīt) 明亮的；伶俐的
bring (briŋ) 帶來
broke (brōk) 斷裂(過去式)；沒錢了
brook (brook) 小河
broom (brōōm) 掃把
brother (bruth'ər) 兄弟
brush (brush) 刷子
bubble (bub'əl) 泡沫
buckle (buk'əl) 環扣
bug (bug) 瓢蟲
bun (bun) 小圓麵包；髻
burn (burn) 燒
bus (bus) 公車
buzz (buz) 嗡嗡叫；門鈴聲
by (bī) 經；沿；依照

Cc

cab (kab) 計程車
cage (kāj) 籠子
cake (kāk) 蛋糕
calendar (kal'ən dər) 日曆；月曆
call (kôl) 叫；打電話
came (kām) 來 (過去式)
camp (kamp) 露營
can (kan) 可以；鐵罐
　　(kən)
candle (kan'dəl) 蠟燭
cane (kān) 手杖
cap (kap) 棒球帽
cape (kāp) 斗篷
car (kär) 汽車
card (kärd) 卡片
care (ker) 關心；在乎
caricature (kar'i kə chər) 諷刺畫
carry (kar'ē) 搬；運；攜帶
cart (kärt) 手推車
cassette (kə set') 錄音帶
cat (kat) 貓
catch (kach) 接；抓住
caught (kôt) 接；抓住 (過去式；過去分詞)
cave (kāv) 洞穴
celery (sel'ər ē) 芹菜
cent (sent) 美元一分
center (sent'ər) 中心

chain (chān) 鐵鍊
chair (cher) 椅子
chalk (chôk) 粉筆
check (chek) 檢查；打勾
cheer (chir) 喝采
cheese (chēz) 起司；乳酪
chess (ches) 西洋棋
chest (chest) 箱子；胸部
chew (chōō) 嚼
chick (chik) 小雞
chicken (chik'ən) 雞；雞肉；膽小
child (chīld) 一個小孩
children (chil'drən) 小孩 (複數)
chimney (chim'nē) 煙囪
chin (chin) 下巴
chip (chip) 薄片
choose (chōōz) 選擇
chopsticks (chäp'stiks') 筷子
chore (chôr) 零工；雜事
church (church) 教堂
circle (sur'kəl) 圓圈
city (sit'ē) 城市
clam (klam) 蛤
clap (klap) 拍手
class (klas) 課；班
claw (klô) 爪子
clean (klēn) 清理；乾淨的
clerk (klurk) 店員
cliff (klif) 懸崖
climb (klīm) 爬
clock (kläk) 時鐘
close (klōz) 關；親密的
clothes (klōz) 衣服
　　(Klōthz)
cloud (kloud) 雲
clown (kloun) 小丑
club (klub) 俱樂部
coat (kōt) 外套
coil (koil) 線圈
coin (koin) 銅板
cold (kōld) 寒冷的；感冒
collar (käl'ər) 領子
college (käl'ij) 學院
collision (kə lizh'ən) 猛烈碰撞
color (kul'ər) 顏色
comb (kōm) 梳子
comic (käm'ik) 漫畫
con (kän) 欺騙；反對
cone (kōn) 甜筒
confusion (kən fyōō'zhən) 疑惑；混亂

Glossary 字彙

congratulation　(kən grach'ə lā'shən)　恭喜
　　　　　　　　(kən graj'ə lā' shən)
　　　　　　　　(kən graj'oo lā' shən)
connect　(kə nekt')　接連
cook　(kook)　廚師；煮
cookie(s)　(kook'ē)　餅乾
cool　(kool)　涼快的；酷的
cooler　(kool-ər)　冰桶
copy　(käp'ē)　影印；複本
cord　(kôrd)　線；電線
cork　(kôrk)　軟木塞
corn　(kôrn)　玉米
cot　(kät)　帆布床；小兒床
cough　(kôf)　咳嗽
could　(kood)　可以 (過去式)
count　(kount)　計算；數一數
cow　(kou)　母牛
coy　(koi)　假裝害羞；靦腆的
crab　(krab)　螃蟹
crack　(krak)　破裂
crane　(krān)　起重機；鶴
crash　(krash)　撞擊
crawl　(krôl)　爬行
crazy　(krā'zē)　瘋狂的
cream　(krēm)　奶脂；乳脂
crew　(kroo)　全體機員；組員
cross　(krôs)　十字架；穿越
crow　(krō)　烏鴉
crowd　(kroud)　群眾
crown　(kroun)　王冠
crush　(krush)　壓碎
crutch　(kruch)　拐杖；支柱
cry　(krī)　哭
cub　(kub)　幼獸
cube　(kyoob)　冰塊；立方體
cuff　(kuf)　袖口
cup　(kup)　有耳杯子
curb　(kurb)　人行道邊石
cure　(kyoor)　治療
cut　(kut)　切
cute　(kyoot)　可愛的
cymbal　(sim'bəl)　鈸

Dd

dad　(dad)　爸爸
dam　(dam)　水壩
dance　(dans)　跳舞
dare　(der)　膽敢；挑戰；敢
dart　(därt)　飛鏢
daughter　(dôt'ər)　女兒

day　(dā)　一天
decision　(dē sizh'ən)　決定
　　　　　(di siah'ən)
deer　(dir)　鹿
decoration　(dek'ə rā'shən)　裝飾
deny　(dē nĭ')　否認
　　　(di nī')
desk　(desk)　書桌
destroy　(di stroi')　毀壞
dew　(doo)　露水
dice　(dīs)　骰子
did　(did)　做 (過去式)
die　(dĭ)　死；一顆骰子
dig　(dig)　挖掘
dim　(dim)　模糊的
dime　(dĭm)　美元十分；一角
direction　(də rek'shən)　方向；說明
　　　　　(dī rek'shən)
dirt　(durt)　塵埃；泥土
dirty　(durt'ē)　髒的
dive　(dīv)　潛水
division　(də vizh'ən)　除以；分開
doctor　(däk'tər)　醫生
dog　(däg)　狗
　　(dôg)
doll　(däl)　洋娃娃
dollar　(däl'ər)　一元
dome　(dōm)　圓頂
donation　(dō nā'shən)　捐贈
door　(dôr)　門
dose　(dōs)　劑量
dot　(dät)　點
dough　(dō)　麵糰
down　(doun)　向下
dragon　(drag'ən)　龍
drape　(drāp)　簾子；帷幕
draw　(drô)　畫
dream　(drēm)　夢
dress　(dres)　洋裝
drew　(droo)　畫 (過去式)
drink　(driŋk)　喝
drip　(drip)　水滴
drive　(drīv)　駕駛
drop　(dräp)　落下
drum　(drum)　鼓
dry　(drī)　乾的；乾燥
duck　(duk)　鴨子
duke　(dook)　公爵

Ee

each　(ēch)　每個

Glossary 字彙

eagle　(ē'gəl)　老鷹
ear　(ir)　耳朵
easy　(ē'zē)　容易的
economical　(ek'ənäm'i kəl)　實惠的；精打細算的
　　　　　　(ē'kə näm'i kəl)
edge　(ej)　邊緣
editor　(ed'it ər)　編輯者
egg　(eg)　蛋
eight　(āt)　八
empty　(emp'tē)　空的；倒空
end　(end)　終止
English　(iŋ'glish)　英語
enjoy　(en joi')　享受
enough　(i nuf')　足夠的
eraser　(ē rā'sər)　擦子
examination　(eg zam'ə nā'shən)　測驗；考試
　　　　　　(ig zam'ə nā'shən)
expiration　(ek'spə rā'shən)　期滿；期限

Ff

face　(fās)　臉
fad　(fad)　一時狂熱
family　(fam'ə lē)　家庭
　　　　(fam'lē)
fan　(fan)　風扇；歌迷；影迷
far　(fär)　遙遠地
fare　(fer)　費用
farm　(färm)　農場
fast　(fast)　快的
fat　(fat)　胖的
fate　(fāt)　命運
father　(fä' thər)　父親
faucet　(fô'sit)　水龍頭
feather　(feth'ər)　羽毛
fed　(fed)　餵 (過去式；過去分詞)
feet　(fēt)　雙腳
fellow　(fel'ō)　同伴
fence　(fens)　籬笆
fern　(furn)　羊齒植物
few　(fyōō)　不多；少的
fig　(fig)　無花果
fight　(fīt)　打架
fin　(fin)　鰭
find　(fīnd)　找到；發現
fine　(fīn)　好的
fire　(fīr)　火
first　(furst)　第一；首先
fish　(fish)　魚
fist　(fist)　拳頭
five　(fīv)　五
flag　(flag)　旗子

flame　(flām)　火焰
flash　(flash)　閃光
flat　(flat)　平坦的；爆胎的
flaw　(flô)　缺陷
flew　(flōō)　飛 (過去式)
flight　(flīt)　飛行；班機
flood　(flud)　洪水
floor　(flôr)　地板
flow　(flō)　流動
flower　(flou'ər)　花
flute　(flōōt)　笛子
fly　(flī)　飛；蒼蠅
focus　(fō'kəs)　焦點；焦距
fog　(fôg)　霧
foil　(foil)　鋁箔紙
fold　(fōld)　摺
fool　(fōōl)　傻瓜
foot　(foot)　一隻腳
for　(fôr)　為了
fork　(fôrk)　叉子
forty　(fôrt'ē)　四十
foul　(foul)　違規的
four　(fôr)　四
fox　(fäks)　狐
frame　(frām)　框子
freckle　(frek'əl)　雀斑
free　(frē)　自由的；免費的；有空的
freeze　(frēz)　凍結
freezer　(frē'zər)　冷凍庫
fresh　(fresh)　新鮮的
fret　(fret)　煩燥；吉他琴格
friend　(frend)　朋友
frighten　(frīt' 'n)　吃驚；驚嚇
frog　(frôg)　青蛙
from　(frum)　從....；由......
front　(frunt)　前面
frown　(froun)　皺眉
fruit　(frōōt)　水果
fry　(frī)　油炸；煎
fudge　(fuj)　一種牛奶軟糖
funny　(fun'ē)　滑稽好笑的
furniture　(fur'ni chər)　家具
fuse　(fyōōz)　保險絲；引信
fuss　(fus)　小題大作；紛擾

Gg

gage　(gāj)　計量器
gain　(gān)　獲得
gale　(gāl)　大風
gamble　(gam'bəl)　賭博
gap　(gap)　裂口

Glossary 字彙

garage (gə räzh') 車庫
　　　 (gə räj')
garden (gärd' 'n) 花園
gate (gāt) 大門
gem (jem) 寶石
general (jen'rəl) 將軍；普遍的
　　　　 (jen'ər əl)
germ (jʉrm) 細菌
gift (gift) 禮物
ginger (jin'jər) 薑
giraffe (jə raf') 長頸鹿
girl (gʉrl) 女孩
glad (glad) 高興的
glance (glans) 瞥見
glass (glas) 玻璃杯；玻璃
glaze (glāz) 上釉；使發亮
glider (glīd'ər) 滑翔機
globe (glōb) 地球儀
glove (gluv) 手套
glue (glōō) 膠水
go (gō) 走；去
goat (gōt) 山羊
gold (gōld) 黃金；金色
gone (gän) 走 (過去分詞)
　　　 (gôn)
good (good) 好的
goose (gōōs) 鵝
grade (grād) 成績
graduation (gra'jōō ā' shən) 畢業
　　　　　　 (gra' jə wā' shən)
grape (grāp) 葡萄
graph (graf) 曲線圖
grasp (grasp) 緊抓住
grass (gras) 草地
gray (grā) 灰色
graze (grāz) 放牧
green (grēn) 綠色
greet (grēt) 打招呼
grew (grōō) 生長 (過去式)
grid (grid) 格子
grill (gril) 烤
grin (grin) 露齒而笑
grind (grīnd) 磨
grip (grip) 握緊；瞭解
gripe (grīp) 抱怨；胃腸絞痛
groom (grōōm) 新郎
grow (grō) 生長；成長；種植
guava (gwä'və) 芭樂
guitar (gi tär') 吉他
gum (gum) 口香糖
gun (gun) 槍
gym (jim) 健身房

Hh
had (had) 有 (過去式；過去分詞)
hair (her) 頭髮
half (haf) 一半
hall (hôl) 走廊
halt (hôlt) 停止
ham (ham) 火腿
hamburger (ham'bʉrg'ər) 漢堡
hand (hand) 手
handle (han'dəl) 把手
handsome (han'səm) 英俊的
　　　　　 (hand' səm)
happy (hap'ē) 快樂的
hard (härd) 硬的；難的
harden (härd' 'n) 變硬
harm (härm) 傷害
harp (härp) 豎琴
has (haz) 有
hat (hat) 有邊帽子
hate (hāt) 恨；厭惡
hay (hā) 乾草堆
head (hed) 頭；朝向
heal (hēl) 治療
hear (hir) 聽
heart (härt) 心
heat (hēt) 熱度
heel (hēl) 鞋後跟
help (help) 幫助
hen (hen) 母雞
herd (hʉrd) 獸群
here (hir) 這裡
　　　 (hēr)
hid (hid) 躲藏 (過去式)
hide (hīd) 躲藏
hind (hīnd) 後面的；臀部
hive (hīv) 蜂巢
hoe (hō) 鋤頭
hoist (hoist) 升起
hold (hold) 握；抱
hood (hood) 車蓋
hoof (hōōf) 蹄
hook (hook) 鉤
hoop (hōōp) 鐵環
hop (häp) 單腳向前跳
hope (hōp) 希望
horn (hôrn) 喇叭
horse (hôrs) 馬
hose (hōz) 水管
hot (hät) 熱的
hot dog (hät dôg) 熱狗
hound (hound) 獵犬

Glossary 字彙

house (hous) 房子
how (hou) 如何
hug (hug) 擁抱
huge (hyōōj) 巨大的
hum (hum) 哼；低唱
hurry (hur'ē) 急忙；催促
hut (hut) 茅草屋

Ii

igloo (ig'lōō') 雪冰屋
ill (il) 生病的
important (im pôrt' ' nt) 重要的
in (in) 在....裡面
indulge (in dulj') 縱容
information (in'fər mā'shən) 資訊；資料
ink (iŋk) 墨水
international (in'tər nash'ə nəl) 國際的
　　　　　　(in'tər nash'ə nal')
invitation (in'və tā' shən) 邀請
iron (ī'ərn) 熨斗；鐵
island (ī'lənd) 島
it (it) 它
item (īt'əm) 項目

Jj

jacket (jak'it) 夾克
jam (jam) 果醬
jar (jär) 大口瓶
jaw (jô) 顎
jazz (jaz) 爵士樂
jeep (jēp) 吉普車
jog (jäg) 慢跑
join (join) 結合；加入；參加
joint (joint) 關節
joke (jōk) 笑話；開玩笑
joy (joi) 喜悅
judge (juj) 法官
jug (jug) 有把水罐
juice (jōōs) 果汁
jump rope (jump rōp) 跳繩
June (jōōn) 六月

Kk

kangaroo (kaŋ'gə rōō') 袋鼠
keep (kēp) 保持
kettle (ket' 'l) 水壺
key (kē) 鑰匙
kick (kik) 踢
kin (kin) 家族；血緣關係；親戚
kind (kīnd) 親切的；種類

king (kiŋ) 國王
kiss (kis) 吻
kit (kit) 一組 (工具)
kitchen (kich'ən) 廚房
kite (kīt) 風箏
knack (nak) 竅門；技能；本領
knead (nēd) 搓，揉，捏
knee (nē) 膝蓋
knelt (nelt) 跪下 (過去式；過去分詞)
knew (nōō) 知道 (過去式)
knife (nīf) 刀子
knit (nit) 編織
knob (näb) 門把
knock (näk) 敲
knoll (nōl) 圓丘；土墩
knot (nät) 結；打結
know (nō) 知道
knowledge (näl'ij) 知識
knuckle (nuk'əl) 手指關節
koala (kō ä'lə) 無尾熊

Ll

lack (lak) 缺少
ladder (lad'ər) 梯子
lady (lād'ē) 女士
lag (lag) 落後；發展緩慢
lake (lāk) 湖
lamb (lam) 小綿羊
lamp (lamp) 檯燈
land (land) 土地；降落
large (lärj) 大的
lark (lärk) 百靈鳥；雲雀
last (last) 最後的
late (lāt) 遲到的；晚的
laugh (laf) 笑
law (lô) 法律
leaf (lēf) 葉子
leather (leth'ər) 皮革
leg (leg) 腿
legislature (lej'is lā' chər) 立法機關
leisure (lē'zhər) 閒暇；休閒
let (let) 讓；允許
life (līf) 生活
light (līt) 燈；淺色的；輕的
like (līk) 喜歡
line (līn) 線條
lion (lī'ən) 獅子
lip (lip) 唇
list (list) 名單；明細
literature (lit'ər ə choor') 文學

Glossary 字彙

little   (lit' 'l)   小的；少許的
live   (liv)   居住；現場直播的
loaf   (lōf)   一條麵包
location   (lō kā'shən)   位置
lock   (läk)   鎖
log   (läg)   圓木材
        (lôg)
long   (lôŋ)   長的
look   (look)   看
lot   (lät)   許多的；場地
loud   (loud)   高聲的
love   (luv)   愛
loyal   (loi'əl)   忠貞的

Mm

mad   (mad)   瘋狂的；憤怒的
made   (mād)   做；使 (過去式；過去分詞)
maid   (mād)   女僕
mail   (māl)   郵件；郵寄
make   (māk)   做；使
male   (māl)   男性
mall   (môl)   購物中心
man   (man)   一個男人
manage   (man'ij)   經營
map   (map)   地圖；繪製地圖
marble   (mär'bəl)   大理石；彈珠
march   (märch)   行進；進行曲
marker   (märk'ər)   麥克筆；白板筆
mat   (mat)   踏腳墊
match   (mach)   火柴
mature   (mə choor')   成熟
measure   (mezh'ər)   測量
meat   (mēt)   肉類
meet   (mēt)   遇見
men   (men)   男人 (複數)
mermaid   (mur'mād')   美人魚
mess   (mes)   雜亂
message   (mes'ij)   信息
met   (met)   見過 (過去式；過去分詞)
mice   (mīs)   老鼠 (複數)
middle   (mid' 'l)   中間
might   (mīt)   可能；可以；強權
milk   (milk)   牛奶
mind   (mīnd)   心智
mirage   (mi räzh')   海市蜃樓
mirror   (mir'ər)   鏡子
miss   (mis)   錯過；想念
mite   (mīt)   蟎蟲
mix   (miks)   混合
mixture   (miks' chər)   混合物
moist   (moist)   潮濕的

mold   (mōld)   模子；黴菌
Mom   (mäm)   媽媽
money   (mun'ē)   錢
monkey   (muŋ'kē)   猴子
moo   (mōō)   牛叫
moon   (mōōn)   月亮
mop   (mäp)   拖把；拖地
mope   (mōp)   鬱悶不樂；自怨自艾
more   (môr)   更多
mother   (muth'ər)   母親
mouse   (mous)   一隻老鼠
mouth   (mouth)   嘴；口
mud   (mud)   泥
mug   (mug)   馬克杯
mule   (myōōl)   騾子
murmur   (mur'mər)   喃喃自語
my   (mī)   我的

Nn

nail   (nāl)   釘子；指甲
name   (nām)   姓名
nap   (nap)   小睡
nation   (nā'shən)   國家
nature   (nā'chər)   自然
naughty   (nôt'ē)   頑皮的
need   (nēd)   需要
needle   (nēd' 'l)   針
nest   (nest)   鳥巢
net   (net)   網子
night   (nīt)   夜晚
nine   (nīn)   九
nod   (näd)   點頭
noise   (noiz)   噪音
noisy   (noiz'ē)   喧鬧的
noodle(s)   (nōōd' 'l)   麵
noon   (nōōn)   中午
nose   (nōz)   鼻子
not   (nät)   不；末；非
note   (nōt)   字條；留言
number   (num'dər)   數字
nurse   (nurs)   護士
nut   (nut)   核果

Oo

ocean   (ō'shən)   海洋
off   (äf)   除掉；離開的
        (ôf)
oil   (oil)   油
on   (än)   在上；論及
one   (wun)   一

Glossary 字彙

open (ō'pən) 打開
orange (ôr'inj) 柳橙
organ (ôr'gən) 風琴；器官
over (ō'vər) 在上；越過
owl (oul) 貓頭鷹
ox (äks) 牛

Pp
pad (pad) 墊料；打印台
page (pāj) 頁
pail (pāl) 提桶
paint (pānt) 著色；粉刷；顏料
pale (pāl) 蒼白的
pan (pan) 平底鍋
pardon (pärd''n) 寬恕
pasture (pas'chər) 牧場
pat (pat) 輕拍
patch (pach) 補綻；補綴
path (path) 小徑
paw (pô) 腳掌 (動物的)
pawn (pôn) 抵押；兵；卒 (西洋棋)
pea (pē) 碗豆
peach (pēch) 桃子
peak (pēk) 山頂；峰
pear (per) 梨子
peel (pēl) 剝皮
peep (pēp) 窺視
pen (pen) 筆
pencil (pen'səl) 鉛筆
people (pē'pəl) 人類
pep (pep) 精力
pet (pet) 寵物；摸
phone (fōn) 電話
phonics (fän'iks) 自然發音法
photo (ō'tō) 照片
piano (pē an'ō) 鋼琴
pick (pik) 挑選
pickle (pik'əl) 醃菜；醃黃瓜
picture (pik'chər) 照片；畫
pie (pī) 派
pig (pig) 豬
pill (pil) 藥丸
pillow (pil'ō) 枕頭
pin (pin) 別針
pine (pīn) 松樹
pink (piŋk) 粉紅色
pip (pip) 種子；籽
pipe (pīp) 煙斗
pitch (pich) 投球
pitcher (pich'ər) 大水罐；投手
pizza (pēt'sə) 比薩

plan (plan) 計畫
planet (plan'it) 星球
plank (plaŋk) 厚板
plant (plant) 植物；種植
plate (plāt) 淺盤子
play (plā) 玩
pleasure (plezh'ər) 愉快
pledge (plej) 誓約
plough (plou) 犁；耕作
plug (plug) 插頭
plum (plum) 梅子
plus (plus) 加；和
point (point) 指向
poison (poi'zən) 毒藥
pool (pōōl) 游泳池
poor (poor) 貧窮的
pop (päp) 流行；爆裂
population (päp'yōō lā'shen) 人口
　　　　　(päp'yə lā'shen)
porch (pôrch) 門廊；玄關
port (pôrt) 港口
pot (pät) 鍋
pouch (pouch) 小袋
practice (prak'tis) 練習
praise (prāz) 讚美
prank (praŋk) 惡作劇
pray (prā) 祈禱
preach (prēch) 傳教
present (prez'ənt) 禮物
　　　　(prē zent') 呈現
pretty (prit'ē) 漂亮的
pretzel (pret'səl) 椒鹽脆餅乾
price (prīs) 價格
prince (prins) 王子
princess (prin'sis) 公主
　　　　　(prin' ses')
print (print) 印刷
prison (priz'ən) 監獄
prisoner (priz'nər) 囚犯
　　　　　(priz'ən ər)
prize (prīz) 獎品
propeller (prə pel'ər) 螺旋槳
　　　　　(prō pel'ər)
prowl (proul) 潛行
pup (pup) 小狗
purse (purs) 錢包
puzzle (puz'əl) 拼圖；迷惑；字謎

Qq
quack (kwak) 鴨叫；庸醫

Glossary 字彙

quality (kwäl'ə tē) 品質
　　　　(kwôl'i tē)
quarter (kwôrt'ər) 美元25分
queen (kwēn) 女王
question (kwes'chən) 問號；問題
quick (kwik) 迅速的
quiet (kwī'ət) 安靜的
quilt (kwilt) 棉被
quit (kwit) 辭職

Rr
rabbit (rab'it) 兔子
rack (rak) 工具架
racket (rak'it) 球拍
rain (rān) 雨
rainbow (rān bō) 彩虹
raise (rāz) 養育；舉起
rake (rāk) 耙子
ran (ran) 跑 (過去式)
range (rānj) 山脈；範圍；系列
rap (rap) 輕敲；饒舌音樂
raw (rô) 生的
reach (rēch) 到達；達成
red (red) 紅色
relation (ri lā 'shən) 關聯；關係
reply (ri plī') 答覆
reservation (rez'ər vā'shen) 預訂
responsibility (ri spän'sə bil'ə tē) 責任
revenge (ri venj') 復仇
rice (rīs) 米飯
rich (rich) 富有的
rid (rid) 除去
ride (rīd) 騎
ridge (rij) 山脊
right (rīt) 正確的；右邊
ring (riŋ) 戒指
rip (rip) 撕破
road (rōd) 道路
rob (räb) 搶劫
robe (rōb) 浴袍
rock (räk) 石頭
rod (räd) 釣竿
rode (rōd) 騎 (過去式)
role (rōl) 角色
roll (rōl) 滾動
roof (rōōf) 屋頂
room (rōōm) 房間
root (rōōt) 根
rope (rōp) 繩子
rose (rōz) 玫瑰
Ross (rôs) 羅斯 (人名)

rough (ruf) 粗糙的
round (round) 圓形的
rub (rub) 摩擦；搓；揉
ruler (rōōl'ər) 尺
run (run) 跑

Ss
sabotage (sab'ə täzh') 破壞
sad (sad) 傷心；難過的
sage (sāj) 聖人
sail (sāl) 帆
sailor (sāl'ər) 船員
sale (sāl) 出售；拍賣
salt (sôlt) 鹽
sand (sand) 沙子
sandwich (san'wich') 三明治
　　　　　(san'dwich')
sap (sap) 樹液
sat (sat) 坐 (過去式；過去分詞)
sauce (sôs) 醬汁
saucer (sô'sər) 碟子
sausage (sô'sij) 香腸
saw (sô) 鋸子；看見 (過去式)
say (sā) 說出
scale (skāl) 天秤
scan (skan) 掃描
scar (skär) 疤
scare (sker) 嚇唬；嚇到
scarf (skärf) 圍巾
school (skōōl) 學校
scissors (siz'ərs) 剪刀
scold (skōld) 罵
score (skôr) 分數
scout (skout) 偵察；童子軍
scowl (skoul) 怒目而視
scrape (skrāp) 刮掉
scratch (skrach) 抓癢
scream (skrēm) 尖叫
screen (skrēn) 螢幕
screw (skrōō) 螺絲釘
screwdriver (skrōō drī'vər) 螺絲起子
scrub (scrub) 擦洗；刷洗
sea (sē) 海
seal (sēl) 海狗
seam (sēm) 縫
seat (sēt) 座位
see (sē) 看見
seem (sēm) 看以；似乎是
seen (sēn) 看見 (過去分詞)
servant (sʉr'vənt) 僕人
seven (sev'ən) 七

Glossary 字彙

shade (shād) 蔭涼處；畫陰影
shadow (shad'ō) 影子；陰影
shall (shal) 應該
shark (shärk) 鯊魚
shave (shāv) 刮鬍子
shawl (shôl) 披肩
she (shē) 她
sheep (shēp) 綿羊
sheet (shēt) 一張；床、被單
shelf (shelf) 架子
shell (shel) 貝殼
ship (ship) 船
shirt (shʉrt) 襯衫
shoe (shoo) 鞋子
shook (shook) 搖動 (過去式)
shop (shäp) 商店；購物
shopkeeper (shäp'kē'pər) 店主
short (shôrt) 短的；矮的
shorts (shôrts) 短褲
shot (shät) 射擊 (過去式；過去分詞)
should (shood) 應該
shoulder (shōl'dər) 肩膀
shout (shout) 呼喊；大叫
shower (shou'ər) 淋浴；陣雨
shrew (shroo) 悍婦；潑婦
shrimp (shrimp) 蝦子
sick (sik) 生病的
signature (sig'nə chər) 簽字；簽名
simple (sim'pəl) 簡單的
sing (siŋ) 唱歌
sink (siŋk) 水槽；下沉
sit (sit) 坐
site (sīt) 地點
six (siks) 六
skate (skāt) 溜冰鞋；溜冰
sketch (skech) 素描
skill (skil) 技巧
skip (skip) 略過
skirt (skʉrt) 裙子
skit (skit) 幽默短劇、短文
skull (skul) 頭蓋骨
skunk (skuŋk) 臭鼬
sky (skī) 天空
slave (slāv) 奴隸
sled (sled) 遊戲用小型雪車
sleep (slēp) 睡覺
sleet (slēt) (下)雨雪；(下)凍雨
sleeve (slēv) 袖子
sleigh (slā) 雪橇
slew (sloo) 殺害 (過去式)
slice (slīs) 薄片；切片
slide (slīd) 滑；滑梯

slip (slip) 滑倒
slot (slät) 投幣口
slow (slō) 慢的
small (smôl) 小的
smart (smärt) 精明的
smell (smel) 聞
smile (smīl) 微笑
smirk (smʉrk) 傻笑
smog (smäg) 煙霧
smoke (smōk) 煙
smooth (smooth) 光滑的
snack (snak) 點心
snail (snāl) 蝸牛
snake (snāk) 蛇
sneak (snēk) 偷偷摸摸
sneaker (snē'kər) 膠底鞋
snore (snôr) 打鼾
snout (snout) 豬隻口鼻
snow (snō) 雪
snowman (snō man') 雪人
soap (sōp) 肥皂
sock (säk) 襪子
soil (soil) 土壤
solar (sō'lər) 太陽的
sold (sōld) 賣 (過去式；過去分詞)
sole (sōl) 唯一的
soon (soon) 不久；即刻
soothe (sooth) 撫慰
soul (sōl) 靈魂
sound (sound) 聲音；鳴響
sour (sour) 酸的
south (south) 南方的
spaghetti (spə get'ē) 義大利麵
spar (spär) 毆鬥
spare (sper) 備用的；免除；撥出
spark (spärk) 火花
speak (spēk) 說話
spear (spir) 矛；魚叉
spice (spīs) 香料
spider (spī' dər) 蜘蛛
spin (spin) 紡紗；快速旋轉
splash (splash) 水花
spleen (splēn) 脾臟
split (split) 劈開
spoil (spoil) 弄壞；寵壞
spool (spool) 捲軸
spoon (spoon) 湯匙
sport (spôrt) 運動
sprain (sprān) 扭傷
spray (sprā) 噴霧
spread (spred) 展開
spring (spriŋ) 彈簧；春天

Glossary 字彙

sprint (sprint) 短跑
sprout (sprout) 芽
spy (spī) 間諜;偵察
square (skwer) 正方形
squash (skwôsh) 壓扁
squat (skwät) 盤坐;蹲
squeak (skwēk) 唧唧叫;軋軋聲
squirrel (skwur'əl) 松鼠
squirt (skwurt) 噴出
stage (stāj) 舞台
stair (ster) 樓梯
stall (stôl) 攤位;熄火;故意拖延
stamp (stamp) 郵票
stand (stand) 站立
star (stär) 星星
stare (ster) 瞪視
start (stärt) 開始
station (stā'shən) 車站
stay (stā) 停留
steeple (stē'pəl) 尖塔
stink (stiŋk) 臭味
stir (stur) 攪動
stone (stōn) 石頭
stool (stōōl) 凳子
stop (stäp) 停止
store (stôr) 商店;貯存
stork (stôrk) 白鸛
stove (stōv) 火爐;瓦斯爐
straight (strāt) 筆直的;正直的
strain (strān) 拉緊;濾乾水份;損傷
strand (strand) 一串;擱淺
strange (strānj) 奇怪的
straw (strô) 吸管;稻草
strawberry (strô ber'ē) 草莓
stream (strēm) 小河;溪流
stress (stres) 強調;壓力
string (striŋ) 細繩;線
strip (strip) 剝光
stripes (strīps) 條紋
stroke (strōk) 一擊
strong (strôŋ) 強壯的
student (stōōd''nt) 學生
study (stud'ē) 學習
sub (sub) 替代;後補
sugar (shoog'ər) 糖
sun (sun) 太陽
supervision (sōō'pər vizh'ən) 督導;監督
swamp (swämp) 沼澤
swam (swam) 游泳(過去式)
swan (swän) 天鵝
swear (swer) 發誓;咒罵;詛咒

sweat (swet) 流汗
sweater (swet'ər) 毛衣
sweep (swēp) 打掃
sweet (swēt) 甜的
swim (swim) 游泳
swing (swiŋ) 鞦韆
switch (swich) 開關

Tt
table (tā'bəl) 桌子
tack (tak) 圖汀
tag (tag) 吊牌;標籤
tail (tāl) 尾巴
take (tāk) 拿;取;搭
tale (tāl) 故事
tall (tôl) 高的
talk (tôk) 談話
tan (tan) 曬黑
tank (taŋk) 坦克車;大槽
tap (tap) 輕敲
tape (tāp) 膠帶
tardy (tär'dē) 遲鈍的
target (tär'git) 目標
tart (tärt) 果子餡餅
taught (tôt) 教 (過去式;過去分詞)
teacher (tē'chər) 老師
team (tēm) 隊;組
teeth (tēth) 一排牙齒
television (tel'ə vizh'ən) 電視
ten (ten) 十
temperature (tem'pər ə chər) 溫度
(tem' prə chər)
tent (tent) 帳棚;帳篷
termite (tur'mīt') 白蟻
test (test) 測驗
thank (thaŋk) 謝謝
that (that) 那個
the (thə) 此;這
(thē)
there (ther) 那兒;那裡
these (thēz) 這些
they (thā) 他們
thick (thik) 厚的
thin (thin) 瘦的;薄的
think (thiŋk) 想
thirsty (thurs'tē) 口渴的
thirteen (thur'tēn') 十三
thirty (thurt'ē) 三十
this (this) 這個
thorn (thôrn) 刺;棘

61

Glossary 字彙

those (thōz) 那些
thread (thred) 線；紗 (縫衣用)
threat (thret) 威脅
three (thrē) 三
threw (throō) 拋；投 (過去式)
throw (thrō) 拋；投
thumb (thum) 拇指
tick (tik) 扁蝨；滴答聲
tie (tī) 領帶
tile (tīl) 瓷磚
tip (tip) 尖端
tire (tīr) 輪胎
tit (tit) 一種鳥類；山雀
to (toō) 向；到；對
toad (tōd) 蟾蜍
toe (tō) 腳趾
toilet (toi'lit) 馬桶
told (tōld) 告訴 (過去式；過去分詞)
tomb (toōm) 墳墓
tone (tōn) 音調
too (toō) 也；太
took (took) 拿；取 (過去式)
tool (toōl) 工具
tooth (toōth) 一顆牙齒
      (toōth)
top (täp) 陀螺；頂端
torch (tôrch) 火把
tough (tuf) 強硬的
towel (tou'əl) 毛巾
town (toun) 市鎮
toy (toi) 玩具
track (trak) 鐵軌；跑道；追蹤
tractor (trak'tər) 農耕機；牽引機
trade (trād) 貿易；交換
trail (trāl) 小道；蹤跡
train (trān) 火車；訓練
tramp (tramp) 踐踏
trap (trap) 陷阱
trash (trash) 垃圾
treasure (trezh'ər) 寶藏
tree (trē) 樹
triangle (trī'aŋ'gəl) 三角形
trip (trip) 旅行；絆倒
tripod (trī'päd') 三角架
trophy (trō'fē) 獎杯
Troy (troi) 特洛依城
truck (truk) 卡車
trunk (truŋk) 樹幹；行李箱；象鼻
try (trī) 試
tub (tub) 浴缸
tube (toōb) 管子
tug (tug) 拉；拖

tune (toōn) 曲調；調音
turkey (tur'kē) 火雞
turn (turn) 轉
turnip (tur'nip) 大頭菜；蕪菁
turtle (turt''l) 烏龜
twelve (twelv) 十二
twig (twig) 細枝
two (toō) 二

Uu

umbrella (um brel'ə) 雨傘
under (un'dər) 在...下面
unfortunately (un fôr'chə nit lē) 不幸地
university (yoōn'ə vur'sə tē) 大學
up (up) 向上
use (yoōz) 使用
    (yoōs)

Vv

vacation (vā kā'shən) 度假；假期
         (və kā'shən)
Valentine's Day (val'ən tīn's -dā) 情人節
van (van) 箱型車
vase (vās) 花瓶
vegetable (vech'tə bəl) 蔬菜
          (vej'tə bəl)
vendor (ven'dər) 小販
vest (vest) 背心
vine (vīn) 藤蔓
violin (vī'ə lin') 小提琴
vision (vizh'ən) 視力；視覺
volcano (väl kā'nō) 火山
vowel (vou'əl) 母音

Ww

wage (wāj) 工資
wait (wāt) 等待
wake (wāk) 醒來
walk (wôk) 走路
wall (wôl) 牆壁
want (wänt) 要
wash (wäsh) 洗
     (wôsh)
watch (wäch) 手錶；注意；看
weak (wēk) 弱的
weather (wethər) 天氣
web (web) 蜘蛛網

Glossary 字彙

wedge (wej) 楔子；三角木；三角形物

weed (wēd) 雜草

week (wēk) 一週

well (wel) 井；好地

west (west) 西方(的)

whale (hwāl) 鯨
(wāl)

what (hwut) 什麼
(wut)

wheat (hwēt) 小麥
(wēt)

wheel (hwēl) 輪子
(wēl)

when (hwen) 何時；當…
(wen)

where (hwer) 哪裡
(wer)

whether (hweth'ər) 是否
(weth'ər)

which (which) 哪一個
(wich)

whip (hwip) 鞭子
(wip)

whirl (hwʉrl) 旋轉
(wʉrl)

whisk (hwisk) 打蛋器
(wisk)

whisker (hwis'kər) 動物的鬍鬚
(wis'kər)

whiskey (hwis'kē) 威士忌
(wis'kē)

whisper (hwis'pər) 耳語；小聲說
(wis'pər)

whistle (hwis'əl) 哨子
(wis'əl)

white (hwīt) 白色
(wīt)

whiz (hwiz) 颼颼聲；青年才俊
(wiz)

wife (wīf) 妻子

will (wil) 將；意志

win (win) 贏

window (win'dō) 窗戶

wish (wish) 意欲；願望

witch (wich) 女巫

with (with) 具有；與；關於
(with)

woman (woom'ən) 一個女人

won (wun) 贏 (過去式；過去分詞)

wood (wood) 樹林；木

would (wood) 將會

wrack (rak) 破壞

wrap (rap) 包裝

wrath (rath) 狂怒

wreath (rēth) 花圈

wreck (rek) 殘骸

wrench (rench) 扳鉗

wrestle (res'əl) 角力

wring (riŋ) 扭；擰

wrinkle (riŋ'kəl) 皺紋

wrist (rist) 手腕

writ (rit) 令狀

write (rīt) 寫

wrong (rôŋ) 錯的

wrote (rōt) 寫 (過去式)

Xx

X-ray (eks'rā') X光

Yy

yard (yärd) 庭院

yarn (yärn) 紗；毛線

yawn (yôn) 打呵欠

yell (yel) 呼喊

yellow (yel'ō) 黃色

yesterday (yes'tər dā') 昨天

yolk (yōk) 蛋黃

yo-yo (yō'-yō') 溜溜球

Zz

zebra (zē'brə) 斑馬

zero (zir'ō) 零
(zē'rō)

zipper (zip'ər) 拉鍊

zoo (zo͞o) 動物園

The Pyramid Method

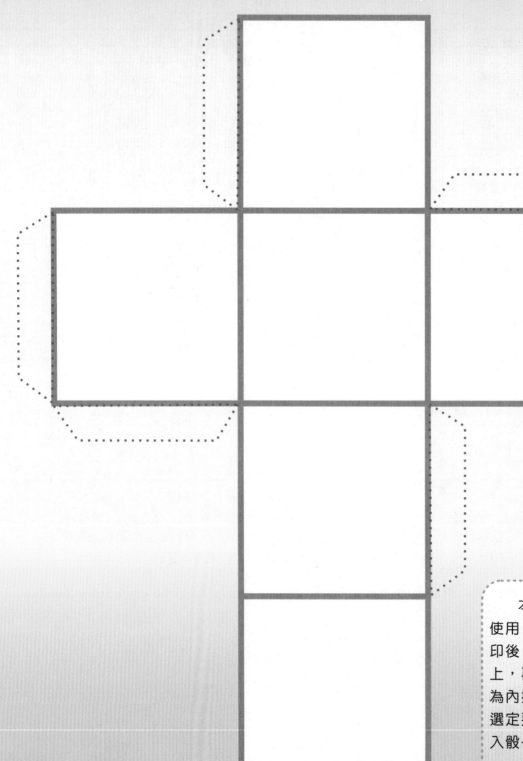

本頁可供影印（放大）使用，請勿直接撕下。影印後，將它黏貼在厚紙板上，再沿線剪下來，虛線為內摺的黏貼部分。再將選定要練習的6個發音填入骰子面。

The Pyramid Method
賓 果 時 間
BINGO!

本頁可供影印使用,請勿直接撕下。本書提供可填入16或25個發音之賓果卡,
可隨練習時間長短做選擇。再將選定要練習的音填入,就可以開始玩賓果遊戲了。

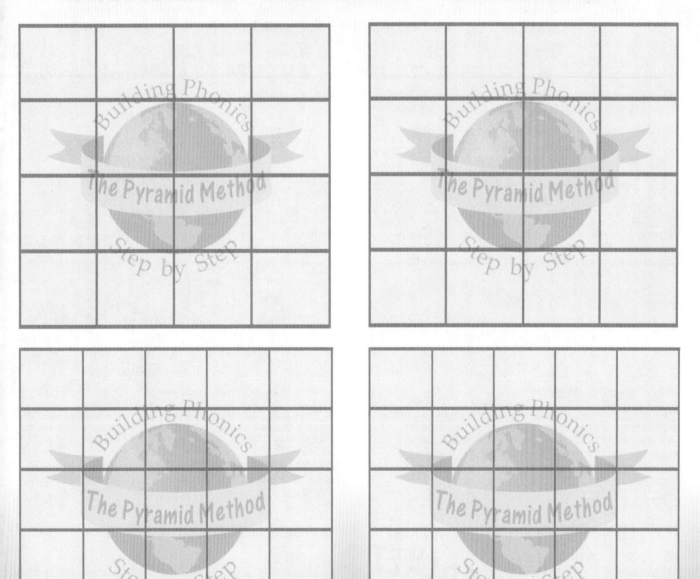